According to findyouronetruelove.com, the current "book" place (so says Gina) to go on the Internet for relationship advice, here are some hot tips on how to respond during a chance meeting with your One True Love.

1. Smile and say, "Hello."
2. Introduce a topic of conversation that you know will be of interest to the object of your desire.
3. Listen to what he says with interest.
4. Laugh at his jokes.

Nowhere does it say you should:

1. Mumble, "Hmffph," in an I-am-an-idiot-I-can-barely-put-two-words-together kind of way, thereby giving him the impression that you are, in fact, a total idiot who cannot put two words together.
2. Put a hand to your mouth, hold on to your stomach (which is queasy due to developing weird powers) with the other, and make a quick dash to the nearest bathroom, thereby giving your loved one the impression that the mere sight of him makes you sick.

But that's exactly what I did after Joe spoke to me.

ALMOST FABULOUS

Michelle Radford

HARPER TEEN

An Imprint of HarperCollins*Publishers*

HarperTeen is an imprint of HarperCollins Publishers.

Almost Fabulous

Copyright © 2008 by Michelle Cunnah
www.harperteen.com

Library of Congress Cataloging-in-Publication Data
Radford, Michelle.

Almost fabulous / Michelle Radford. — 1st ed.

p. cm.

Summary: When she discovers that she has extrasensory
powers, fourteen-year-old Fiona finds it increasingly difficult to
remain anonymous and lead a quiet trouble-free life, unnoticed
by the school's bully.

ISBN 978-0-06-125235-8 (pbk. bdg.)

[1. Extrasensory perception—Fiction. 2. Bullies—Fiction.
3. Self-confidence—Fiction. 4. Interpersonal relations—
Fiction. 5. Single-parent families—Fiction. 6. High schools—
Fiction. 7. Schools—Fiction. 8. London (England)—Fiction.
9. England—Fiction.] I. Title.

PZ7.R1174Alm 2008   2007018378
[Fic]—dc22   CIP
                                                                AC

Typography by Ray Shappell

First Edition

For Thomas and Gracie

ALMOST FABULOUS

Prologue

Not that I'm some kind of total Predictable Routine Freak or anything, but I figure that with my mum moving us every year or so until I was eleven I've had enough change and chaos in my fourteen years of life to last until I'm, oh, at least a hundred and fifty.

Sadly today when I climb out of bed at six to begin my Predictable Routine I have no inkling, none whatsoever, that Predictable is about to fly out the window and my life will never be the same again.

Chapter 1

Just like every morning, I scan the newspapers online, which is no more depressing than usual as they're always full of either global warming, or murders, or natural disasters, or drug barons and gangland wars, and then I switch to the financial reports to cheer myself up because these are the parts I like best.

And if I find something that *really* interests me, like this one about Funktech, an American company that makes really cool electronic stuff, I print out the information so that I can either add it to my information dossier or research it later.

I know. I'm not your usual fourteen-year-old.

But today I don't put this particular article away for later, I read it *right now* because I'm getting a little prickle at the back of my neck. Just a little tingly kind of feeling. And as I read that Funktech has recently expanded into Britain, in fact into London, the tingly feeling gets even stronger. Like I should check out Funktech's website immediately.

I get these little tingly kind of feelings from time to time—call it female intuition or something. Like when Mr. Fenton, our math teacher, went on the school ski trip—I just had that tingly feeling that he might break his leg on the nursery slope if he went, and he did. Which was a total disaster because we had to have Mr. Sharpe for math the whole of the term and he made us study boring stuff like geometry, which we'd already covered, instead of interesting stuff like quadratic equations.

Or like sometimes I get that tingly feeling that I might bump into Mean Melissa Stevens, Her Royal Hotness and Local Menace, if I take my usual route to school on a certain day because that would be another total disaster. So I leave home earlier and walk the long way instead. Or when I'm actually at school and Melissa is around, and I'm wishing for her not to notice me. I mean, when I keep a low profile (most of the time), the low-level fear and the tingle seem to go hand in hand.

But that tingly feeling can also be a good thing.

Like when I'm checking the financial pages, that tingly feeling might mean that I've found a great company to invest in, which is quite unusual for someone of fourteen, I suppose. Investing, I mean, not the intuition thing. Although some people might think that the intuition thing is a bit odd as well. Which is why I haven't told anyone about it.

So I follow my instincts and load Funktech's URL, but then, when I click on the About Us page, the tingly feeling becomes a huge prickle.

The CEO is called William Brown, which is my dad's name.

Not that I have ever actually met my dad.

Mum lost him, oh, about twelve hours after my conception.

When I say "lost him," I don't mean he's dead, I mean lost him in a losing-someone-and-not-being-able-to-find-them-ever-again kind of way.

Yes, that sounds a bit careless, but it really wasn't Mum's fault. See, she met him at this huge annual music festival (which is held in a field at a place called Glastonbury), and it was Love At First Sight. And because it was a music festival and there was a lot of emotion running high, Mum and my father got a bit carried away (which is how I came to exist).

Unfortunately at the end of the festival there was a huge riot (leading to 235 arrests and fifty thousand pounds' worth of damage), and Mum and William Brown got separated in The Chaos That Ensued.

Mum couldn't find him again afterward because they hadn't gotten as far as swapping addresses—so wrapped up in the music and so much in love were they. They did, however, swap names, which is a relief, because it's important for a girl to have her father's name on her birth certificate.

I don't think Mum's ever gotten over her William Brown, though, because sometimes, when she thinks I'm not paying attention, she sighs and looks sad as she takes out the old photo one of her friends took of them at the festival. It's a bit fuzzy and you can't really see him that clearly. But you can see that he's tall, and gangly, and handsome, and has long dark hair. You can see his eyes, too, and they look kind and twinkly.

Mum says that I have his eyes. Which is nice, because I don't take after him at all in the tall, handsome department. I don't take after Mum in the beautiful department, either.

Perhaps I'll add this William Brown to my William Brown file, which currently has 463 people in it, winnowed down from the 17.9 million pages you get on Google when you search "William Brown." (Why does my dad have to have such a common name?!) I've never done anything with the file because none of the William Browns seem as if they could be *our* William Brown—it's just comforting to keep ruling out the wrong ones. My years of William Brown research have proven that the chances of this William Brown being *my* William Brown are totally improbable. Nevertheless there is a Meet Our CEO page on the Funktech website, so I might as well go ahead and "meet" him. And when I do go ahead and Meet Our CEO, there is a photo of him, and the huge prickle becomes a loud, deafening roar like so much radio static buzzing in my ears.

The first thing I notice is that his hair is dark brown. But not long, so if he is my William Brown then he has obviously had a haircut. That's to be expected in fifteen years.

The second thing I notice are his kind, brown, twinkly eyes.

The third thing I notice really freaks me out.

As I watch, the photo on my screen solidifies into a 3-D image, which gives me a shock, but I haven't seen the real party trick yet.

Just as I am thinking, *Wow, those people at Funktech are really out there with technology,* the 3-D image becomes real. Not like someone on TV being real, but *really* real, almost as if

William Brown has suddenly pushed his head through the computer screen and is in my bedroom. And what's more, William Brown's mouth curves into a smile, and then his lips move as if he is going to speak to me. And then he does speak to me.

"Don't be afraid," William Brown tells me.

And even though he has a nice baritone voice and a nice American accent, this is just too freaky.

Before William Brown Talking Head can speak to me any more, I click the box marked X and close down my Internet connection. Then I turn off my laptop and put it in the closet, to be on the safe side.

I am afraid. I am very, very afraid.

By the time I have showered and dressed, as I normally do, my hands have stopped shaking. Nearly.

"What would you do?" I ask the Albert Einstein poster on my bedroom wall. (Fortunately it doesn't answer.)

William Brown Talking Head can't be my William Brown, I tell myself. Although my voice of reason is not listening because it is telling me that (a) he was the right kind of age, and (b) he had the right kind of general look. Especially the kind, twinkly eyes. But (c) Mum never mentioned him being some sort of magician.

I can hear Mum singing as she gets dressed. "It's such a perfect da—ay," she belts out in her deep, scratchy voice. "A perfect day to fall in lo—ove. To fall in love with you——oo." Recently, she's been singing a lot of songs from her Bliss Babes days (the pop group she used to be in). She sings them a lot when she's happy, so why upset her? What if it's not her William Brown? And what if I'm going insane?

By the time I reach the bottom of the stairs, I decide that I will put this William Brown thing in the back of my mind and think about it later. And by the time I reach the kitchen, I decide that the whole talking-head thing was just really, really great technology. That's all. Because, truly, the only other explanation is that I am going insane. Or have a brain tumor. Or possibly both!

Deep breaths, deep breaths.

If I can just switch back to my nice Predictable Routine, all will be well.

Just as usual, Daphne Kat is dying of starvation and rubs herself against my legs, so I feed her a can of something that smells vile but is apparently delicious to cats, and according to the label, nine out of ten of them prefer it to any other cat food. Which always gives me an instant vision of a scientist in a white coat asking ten kitties which do they prefer, Horrible Brand A or Yummy Brand B, and nine out of ten kitties nodding their heads solemnly when he says Yummy Brand B.

It's obvious that Daphne Kat likes it because she always gobbles it down and licks the dish clean like it's going to be the last meal she'll ever get, and after the life of Abandonment and Neglect she had before we adopted her from Rescued Pets she deserves the tastiest cat food money can buy. Although you'd think that after three years of regular meals she'd kind of realize that there would be, you know, a next meal.

Daphne Kat's mind is a mystery to me.

Then, also just like usual, I make breakfast for Mum and me, which consists of a bowl each of bran cereal with skim milk and banana slices, and two cups of decaffeinated tea. See, that's healthy and in view of the fact that she's my only parent, I need to take care of her heart. After all, if something happened to her, what would happen to me? I'd probably have to go and live with Grandmother Elizabeth. Which would be a disaster.

Although perhaps I've just found a father to add to the equation?

"Good morning, darling." Mum breezes in through the kitchen door and kisses the top of my head. "Isn't it a beyoodi-ful day?" She pirouettes around our cheerful cream, yellow, and green kitchen, and I laugh. "A perfect day to fall in lo——ove," she sings, patting Daphne Kat on the head before sitting down opposite me.

I squash that father thought as we sit and chat over break-fast. We do this every morning. I tell her what my plans are—which on Monday and Wednesday (today) involve class, followed by studying with Gina at her house, followed by home. Tuesday and Thursday also involve class, but followed by studying with Gina at my house. Friday involves just going to school, then coming home, because Gina plays poker with her grandfather on Fridays. Then Mum tells me what her plans are—usually which CD she is producing and why Band A is a joy to work with, unlike Artist B who—just between the two of us—is a complete prima donna.

Except she doesn't say that today. Because Mum isn't pro-ducing any CDs today. No, today she is working on a charity concert full of big-name pop stars and some fairly unknown pop stars (to showcase their talent) to raise money for grants to help young musicians.

This is great, this is fantastic, and I am supportive, I really am, because helping others is very important, and Mum knows everyone in the music industry, and she'll work incred-ibly hard behind the scenes to put the project together.

But then I start to get another inkling that today might not be a normal kind of day.

"Fabulous Fiona, I have something exciting to tell you," Mum says, getting serious.

Only Mum calls me Fabulous Fiona. It's a nickname she gave to me when I was a baby. Apparently I walked before most of the other babies, and talked in full sentences before most of the other babies, and learned to read when I was four. Also, I eat a lot (I have a high metabolism), and I'm still skinny. Mum says it must be all the energy I spend thinking about things.

But I must have peaked early because now I am simply boring, normal, nondescript Fiona. Apart from the high IQ thing. Apart from the fact that because I am so literal—too literal sometimes—and don't like change, one doctor thought I was autistic (which I am not). But calling me Fabulous Fiona gives Mum pleasure, so why protest?

"I want you to know that this is just a one-off thing," she continues, looking at me a bit cautiously over her bran and banana slices, then pauses and tilts her head to one side.

She always does this when she's got bad news to tell me, like, "You're going to stay with your grandmother for a few days." Bad news because my grandmother is not a nice person and disapproves of, oh, just about Everyone in the Entire World—especially my mother and therefore by association me. Given a choice of staying with her or running naked down our road, it would be a hard one to call.

"What one-off thing?" I prompt Mum because she's chewing on the bottom corner of her lip; this is also a Sign of Bad News. So now I'm just a bit (actually a lot) anxious.

"The thing is . . . The thing is the Bliss Babes are reuniting—you know—just for this one concert. We are definitely not going to get some idiotic idea in our heads that we should re-form and start cutting CDs in Hamburg, or exploring the music scene in Paris, or touring the world or anything, so don't you worry about moving away and upheaval. Because-theredefinitelywon'tbeanymovingawayandupheaval."

She says the last part really quickly, and I feel all the air whoosh out of my lungs, and I can't help it, I just can't help thinking, *Oh, no, here we go again.* Instead I try for an encouraging smile and say, "That will be great. It will be just like the old days." *But hopefully not too much like the old days,* I think, but do not say aloud.

Okay, so I came out sounding just a bit lame, but I'm doing my best here. Especially after my shock with the William Brown Talking Head. Which I am definitely not going to think about.

Deep breaths. Deep breaths.

"So you're really okay with it?"

"Absolutely," I lie and smile even harder.

Although I'm trying to look happy and normal, Mum, in that sixth-sense sort of way that mothers have, says, "You sure you're okay? Really, I know you like to worry, but don't. Cotch down a bit."

Cotch down a bit?

Mum definitely spends too much time listening to my best friend, Gina, who currently says things like "cotch down" all the time, because Gina's trying to be up on what she deems "überly cool slang."

But mothers shouldn't use such phrases as "cotch down." Mothers should say "chill out" instead, because that's the slang from their own era. Although Gina's mum says, "Don't worry, dear," because she's ancient.

On the other hand, I guess Mum has to keep up with all

the, you know, current phrases on account of working with all those young musicians.

It's kind of cool that my mother is a successful music producer, and writes songs, and wears interesting clothes such as tight leather pants and black leather biker jackets, because a lot of the other mothers are old and wear boring, shapeless dresses and skirts with flowers on them. At least, Gina's mother wears dresses and skirts with flowers on them, but it has to be said—Gina's mum is in her fifties, which is *really* ancient, so therefore boring clothes are okay. And she's nice, in a very motherly kind of way.

Mum's only thirty-five (which is still quite old) and some people think she's pretty hot—at least Mr. Fenton obviously thinks she's hot (as has every other male teacher I've had). I definitely do not like to think of my mother and "hot" in the same sentence, but it is keeping my mind off the real issues.

I am trying very hard not to panic about this morning's events, so I'm thinking of other things to distract me, rather than the fact that William Brown might possibly be *my* William Brown, and how did he do that thing with his head? Or the implications of the Bliss Babes reunion, and how it will probably have a disastrous impact on Mum's only child's life because it will no doubt completely ruin my Predictable Routine.

I don't say any of this to Mum because of not wanting to hurt her feelings and because of not wanting to make her feel lacking and because of trying not to be selfish. As mothers go, mine's fantastic: She's fun, she loves me, and she tries really hard. Especially because I strongly suspect that she gave up the band, and touring, for me. Plus, I know that she feels guilty that she lost my dad before I was born.

I feel instantly guilty. In view of all that Mum's lost in her life, or given up for my sake, the least I can do is be happy for her now.

Although she might not have lost my father in the first place if she'd only told him she was Right Honorable and that her parents were the Baron and Baroness de Plessi, instead of giving her last name as Blount, which is not a lie but is not the whole truth. He could have tracked her down no problem at the de Plessi country estate because it's listed in all the books about the peerage.

But Mum wasn't speaking to Grandmother Elizabeth in those days, because of Mum's Rebel Years—a whole different complicated story that involves her running off to join a band, which eventually turned out pretty well for her. Mum didn't even tell *me* about her family until three years ago, and frankly our lives were a lot less fraught before Mum patched up things with Grandmother Elizabeth.

So when Mum tells me about all the famous stars who have already agreed to give up their time, and she asks me, "Are you worried because the concert's taking place at the Sound Garden and a lot of your school friends will probably be there?" I say, "No, I'm definitely not worried." Even though I definitely am.

What if everyone finds out that my mother is in a band and in a concert with many famous people like the Arctic Monkeys, and Sting, and Madonna, and on TV? I will never be Anonymous Fiona again, which will be very bad indeed. Especially as I've spent years perfecting Total Anonymity, the only way to survive countless new schools and protect myself against Local Menaces like Melissa Stevens.

Especially as my neck begins to tingle.

■ ■ ■

As I walk to school the long way—just in case the neck tingle means an encounter with Mean Melissa and Gang—I think, *Thank goodness it's a sunny June day, instead of a rainy one.* I also think about the implications of Mum's news and the possibility of, oh, finding my long-lost father, as well as my potential Total Insanity or Deadly Brain Tumor, and I am now more than a teeny bit worried.

I don't mean to be selfish and think only of myself. I truly don't. But this is serious!

THINGS I AM CURRENTLY WORRIED ABOUT

- The situation in the Third World.
- World Peace in general.
- The Environment.
- Mean Melissa Stevens and Gang. Because if they hear about the concert—which will be hard to miss seeing as it is taking place practically on the school's doorstep—and if they find out that I'm related to Mum, they'll remember me and they'll do horrible things to me, like grabbing my school bag when I'm on my way home and "accidentally" spilling the contents (including my math homework) into the River Thames, or posting fliers around the school that say I'm in love with, oh, some popular boy like Joe Summers (which I secretly am, but still!), and my life will be *over*.
- Mum reuniting with the Bliss Babes. Because the reunion will be so great that she will immediately want to give up her successful producing career and go on the road with the band again, or live in a foreign country to absorb the

culture of its music, which means that I will have to go on the road with her and live in other countries where I don't even speak the same language as the other kids, start over at lots of schools, and my life will be *over*!

- Or even worse, she'll go on tour with the band and leave me behind with Grandmother Elizabeth, and my life *really* will be *over*!

- William Brown, my long-lost millionaire father, will sue for custody of me and win, and then I'll have to go and live with him in America and I'll never see Mum ever again and my life will *really, really* be *over*!

- Brain tumors, in which case none of the above matters.

However, if everyone at school finds out about Mum and the band, my leaving Elizabeth I High School (lots of schools are named after dead kings of England, but not many are named after dead queens) might be a *good* thing. . . .

On the other hand, I finally have a best friend and I don't want to leave her and start over.

Plus, if I have to move I will never see the love of my life (even though He Will Never Know) ever again. Joe Summers, fifteen-year-old sex god, and brain god, and all-round *god* god. I've never gone so far as to commit to a crush before and now that I have, how will I survive without ever seeing or talking with him again?

I wish I could go back to sleep so I could wake up again, stick to my Predictable Routine and do this morning over, without all the Unpredictable Stuff. Seeing as I don't have the gift of time travel, however, I guess I'll just go to school instead.

Chapter 2

"I think you worry too much," Best Friend Gina tells me by the lockers before homeroom.

"But my life will be over!" I say, a bit dramatically. Clearly Gina hasn't thought through all the implications—especially the one where she loses her best friend on account of the touring.

I haven't mentioned the William Brown Talking Head or the fact that he might be my father, because that sounds totally insane. Instead I have a cunning plan to check out his talking-head photo online again, later when Gina and I are doing our homework in her bedroom. You know, to get her to verify the talking-head part, just in case I do have a terminal brain tumor or something, and am therefore delusional.

"Look, I think it's really book that your mum's in a rock band and is helping young musicians," Gina tells me, totally missing the point. "Mine only nags me about homework. And about eating my green vegetables, because some people in the world don't get enough to eat, and I should be grateful."

I'm thinking that Gina in her status as my best friend should be a bit more supportive. But because I don't understand Gina half of the time these days, I say, "What do you mean by *book*?"

"Book is the new cool," Gina says. "Kieran says it all the time."

Kieran, Kieran, Kieran. Every second word out of her mouth these days is *Kieran*. Kieran is one of the resident jocks and currently Gina's new crush and style guru. He's fifteen (like my secret god, Joe), and therefore, apparently a real man. (He seems okay for a jock—you know, he's not mean to us lesser mortals. I think we don't register on his radar.) But Gina thinks that her love is hopeless because Kieran's preferred type is cute, petite brunettes with blue eyes, like Bev Grainger (one of Melissa Stevens's Gang), instead of tall, lanky, freckled, auburn-haired, green-eyed girls like Gina.

I keep telling Gina that her long auburn hair, and freckles, and green eyes are totally cute, too—which they are—and that she's not lanky, she's athletic, but she just shakes her head and sighs. I haven't told Gina about my Joe Summers secret because Gina's brother, Brian, is best friends with Joe, and it's not that I don't trust Gina with this secret, but there are four very good reasons why I haven't told her.

1. Joe, like me, is around their house a lot, and if Gina knew, she'd treat me differently when he was around and treat him differently when I was around, and then he'd guess, and then my life would be over.

2. Gina would accidentally let something slip to Brian, who would in turn share it with Joe. See 1 (about my life being over).

3. Joe is currently dating Melissa Stevens. I know. It's pretty unbelievable. I don't understand how someone as smart as Joe (both of his parents are scientists!) could be interested in her. But Melissa is completely Sweetness and Light when he's around. She's also the vice president of the Theoretical Stockbroker club (Joe is president), and apart from the fact that she is smart (but not as smart as she thinks she is), she is also gorgeous (unlike me). I mean, gorgeous, interesting Melissa on one hand. Boring, nongorgeous Fiona on the other. No contest.

4. With all the stress in my life at present, do I need more?

"Just think about it," Gina tells me, tugging on my arm. "Look on the bright side. When everyone finds out about the concert, you'll be the most popular girl in the school."

Gina's eyes practically have stars in them. I know what she's thinking. If I become popular, then she, by association, will also be popular, and Kieran will notice her.

"I don't want to be popular," I tell her. "I mean, being popular is just so . . . so cliquey. Then you have to talk like them and act like them."

"I know," she sighs. But not in a disapproving kind of way. In a this-would-be-my-life's-towering-achievement kind of way.

"But it would be a lie. People would only like me because of my mother."

"It would be, you know, supremely mint!" Gina obviously isn't listening to me. I am wasting my breath.

"Mint?" I shake my head. Honestly, doesn't anyone speak real English anymore?

"Yes, you know, cool as in minty cool. Kieran told me about it last night."

I do not point out that Gina reading Kieran's blog every evening does not really amount to him *telling* her about anything. Why ruin her hopes?

I forget all about Kieran and Joe and brain tumors and mint as I spy two of my most unfavorite people heading in our general direction.

"You know what else this concert thing means, though, don't you?" I tell Gina darkly, as Melissa Stevens and Suzy Langton (another of Melissa's Gang) are walking down the corridor with Gaynor Cole. I'm not close enough to hear what they are saying, but they're probably saying awful stuff to Gaynor about her glasses and her acne problem under the pretext of wanting to, you know, "help" her.

"Apart from you being the bookest girl in school?" Gina says.

"No. It will be the end of Total Anonymity! Melissa and Gang will remember that I exist and will find some way to torment me."

"But in your role as most popular kid, they will leave you alone."

Honestly I really can't see that happening. Either part of that statement.

"And in your role as best friend of the most popular kid, they will remember you, too," I say. "Have you forgotten the Geography Project Incident?"

It was two years ago, but the memory is as fresh as yesterday.

It featured me hiding behind the bus shelter because I'd had a prickly feeling and had spotted Melissa and Gang. It also featured Gina just down the street, oblivious to the fact that Melissa and Gang were right behind her.

After they generally tormented Gina by poking her in the back, and kicking at her ankles as she walked, and sniggering horribly, they also relieved Gina of her model farm project. And then they smashed it on the sidewalk and kicked it about like a soccer ball.

There were plastic pigs, and bits of squashed modeling-clay pond, and fake chicken feathers, and Lego farmhouse blocks everywhere. It was a mess. We had to do a quick fix during lunch break in the art room. Gina got a C instead of a B and her mother wasn't very happy about that. It was how Gina and I became friends, though, so I was happy about that part.

"Oh," Gina says, her face falling. And then she spots Melissa and Suzy, too. "I think we should go to our home-rooms right now, yes?"

"Absolutely. See you in history class."

In view of everything that's happened so far, I have forgotten that today is report-card day.

"Fiona," Mr. Fenton, my homeroom (and math) teacher says, as he hands me my report card. "Mediocre, but try harder next term."

Whew. It is such a relief when I open it and find that, yes, I've scored all Bs, except for physical ed, for which I scored an A. But then everyone gets an A for Ms. Maldine's class, because Ms. Maldine is just happy you've turned up.

Being relieved to get Bs, when of course most people would prefer straight As, sounds completely mad. Especially when you have a high IQ like me, but trust me, I have my reasons.

Melissa is an excellent example of why it's important to blend into the background. If you score straight As on your report card and Melissa doesn't (she likes to think of herself as the Brains *and* Beauty of our grade), a teacher might just say, "Melissa, I wish you'd be more like Fiona—she studies hard and always gets an A." Which would be disastrous on the Total Anonymity front. And the bullying front.

"Not bad," Mr. Fenton says as he hands Melissa her report card. "Although you need to work on your chemistry and math. Gaynor," he says, continuing on to the next row, "great work. Straight As as usual."

Nice job, Mr. Fenton, I think. Doesn't he realize that he's just condemned poor Gaynor to more torture later today?

I glance carefully across at Melissa, who I have the misfortune of having in most of my classes, and see her puzzling over her report card. "This can't be right," she whispers to Suzy Langton and Bev Grainger, as she flicks her blond hair over her shoulder. "This just can't be right. *It's a disaster.* Do you realize what this means?"

Suzy Langton, who is not the sharpest knife in the drawer, asks, "That you're not the brightest girl in eighth grade, anymore?" which is a mistake because Melissa scowls.

"No, you idiot," Bev Grainger tells her in a horrified tone. "It means Melissa won't be getting that trip to Manhattan Fashion Week her parents promised her if she got perfect scores! So she won't get inside information on what next spring's hottest looks will be!"

"Oh my God, that's terrible!" Suzy Langton puts her hand to her mouth.

"I *must* go to that show!" Melissa is the picture of tragedy. "I need to go to that show—it would be the pinnacle of my entire life!" Secretly I want to laugh at the expression on their faces, because I can think of far more terrible things than not attending a fashion week.

"Girls, this is homeroom, not social hour," Mr. Fenton says. "Mike, also straight As—you're a credit to the school," he continues, oblivious of the trauma he has just delivered to Melissa's fashion-dedicated heart.

"But, Mr. Fenton," Melissa calls out in her sugariest tone of voice, her face brightening. She's obviously got something up her sleeve. "How come Mike got an A for math and I only got a C? You know we worked together on our project. I think I need to get re-graded. I totally should have the same grade as Mike. It's only fair, don't you think?"

"Melissa, from watching you in math class it was fairly obvious that he did most of the work, while you chatted with Suzy and Bev about the latest lip gloss or coolest mascara. The C I awarded you stands," Mr. Fenton tells her. "As for chemistry, take that up with Mr. Simpkins."

"But I *completely* did my part," Melissa says insistently. "Tell him, Mike," she commands him. "Go on, *tell* him."

It's simply not true that she did her share of the work. Everybody knows that the only reason Melissa asked Fat Mike to be her partner and has been nice to him recently is so that she can improve her math grade and score that Manhattan trip. She's been talking about it nonstop.

"Um," Mike says, going red, because Melissa has that

effect on men. Even though she's been cruel to Mike in the past—I mean, she's the one who gave him the nickname Fat Mike in the first place, back in sixth grade—he's still susceptible to Melissa's feminine charms. "Yes, of course," he agrees with her. "You did. Um, absolutely."

Melissa, Suzy, and Bev smile at one another when he says this, and not in a nice kind of way. I feel sorry for Fat Mike—can't he see that Melissa's just using him? I was once his partner for a math project myself, and you know what? He's a really smart person, and funny, too, once he forgets to be all doom and gloom about everything. That was the only time I ever got an A (apart from physical ed) so, of course, I've avoided doing any kind of project with him ever since.

"Thank you, Mike," Melissa says sweetly, and Suzy and Bev giggle as Fat Mike goes even redder. "Mr. Fenton? Did you hear that?"

Mr. Fenton's not listening, because now that he's handed out all the report cards, he's at the class door and too busy flirting with our geography teacher, Miss Ethelridge, who told us at the beginning of the year that she is definitely a Miss and not a Ms.

So much for the years of women's fight for emancipation, sister.

"Mr. Fenton, did you hear what Mike said?" Melissa tries one more time to get his attention. "About me doing my share of the work?"

"Melissa, my word's final." Mr. Fenton shakes his head, and then re-concentrates on his flirting with Miss Ethelridge. I don't think Melissa is too happy about that because she presses her lips together.

"You should get your dad to complain," Suzy says, shaking her head, which makes her black, curly hair bobble about like a bunch of snakes, and I want to laugh again. "He'll have to listen—your dad's an important sponsor for the new gymnasium. That's just so totally unfair of Mr. Fenton."

"Oh, I'll get my revenge on Mr. Fenton." Melissa's eyes narrow as she says this, which makes her look mean and not beautiful at all. Then she glances across at poor Gaynor Cole, whose only crime was to score perfect As, and I don't want to laugh anymore. My stomach feels queasy.

There are always a few bad eggs in any school and I should know more than most people because I attended quite a few different ones during what I refer to as the Traveling Years with Mum. You have to learn who they are and how to take evasive action and become part of the woodwork. You know— blend into the background and achieve Total Anonymity.

The bell rings, and as we all begin to file out of the classroom for the first period of the day, I am trying to blend into the background and achieve Total Anonymity. It's oddly hard today because I am not as calm and collected as usual, because of William Brown Talking Head.

Then Melissa, Bev, and Suzy practically push some other kids out of the way as they head for Gaynor Cole. Melissa and Suzy both have Post-It notes in their hands, and I suspect that those Post-It notes have something horrible written on them that will upset Gaynor. My stomach gets even more queasy.

This is precisely one of the main reasons why I avoid making lots of friends. Because if they are your friends and you begin to care about them, you find yourself defending them against people like Melissa and that is suicidal. Except for Gina, who despite her occasional yearnings for popularity is also a mistress of blending into the background and achieving Total Anonymity. I taught her well.

But as Gaynor reaches the door, I can't help feeling ashamed and furious and cowardly and powerless, all at the same time. Then I get that prickly feeling at the back of my neck and I know that something bad is going to happen.

"You really should do something about your acne," Melissa tells Gaynor in a faux-friendly voice. "Because that zit on your nose is nearly the size of Jupiter." Then she laughs her tinkly laugh and touches Gaynor on her back as if she's being friendly. But she's not. Her purpose is to stick the Post-It note to Gaynor. It says, *Zit.*

"I wouldn't leave the house with such a disfigurement," Suzy says, laughing along, as she also touches her hand to Gaynor's back. The Post-It note says, *Freak.* Gaynor's face is white with fear.

"If you like I could write down the name of a good epidermist," Melissa continues. "Because let's face it—you could do with all the help you can get."

I really wish that Melissa would just STOP. I really wish it with all my being that the Post-It notes on Gaynor's back would fall on the floor, and Melissa would trip, LOSE HER BALANCE, and MAKE A FOOL OF HERSELF. Just for once, I want the good guy to win. Or rather, not to lose.

As I wish this and remember all the horrible things she has done to so many people, and what a great place this school could actually be if it wasn't for the awful, mean people like her, the prickle becomes a tingle in my brain, getting stronger and stronger as my face burns with anger. I start to see little black spots in front of my eyes. I can hear the peculiar buzzing in my ears again. Just as I think my brain is going to explode from the pressure, the feeling disappears, leaving me completely wrecked, and I stumble.

Then something totally weird happens.

The Post-It notes on Gaynor's back really *do* detach themselves and fall to the floor, and as Melissa reaches out her hand to catch one, she really *does* trip up, knocks into Bev, and falls down on her derriere. Not hard enough to cause fatal derriere damage or anything, but enough to make her yelp.

It can't possibly have been *me* making her trip up, could it? After all, I didn't think the part about her landing on her derriere, did I?

Several brave students, people like Andrea Spencer, who seems to have no fear of anything, laugh. But I don't. As Suzy and Bev help Melissa to her feet, I am so shocked by what has happened that when they turn around to see who might have pushed them, I forget to look innocent, even though I am innocent, because I didn't do anything. *Did I?*

And because I am so busy worrying about this latest incident in my completely wacky day, and the Mum-and-the-Bliss-Babes thing, and the William Brown Talking Head, instead of trying to blend into the background and achieve Total Anonymity, I am standing here with my eyes open wide and, in fact, my mouth open wide, too.

They notice me instantly—possibly because of all the wide-open orifices on my astonished face—and fix their eyes on me in a way that promises Trouble Later. This is bad, this is so bad. After nearly three years of Total Anonymity they're noticing me!

As my heart starts to thud with the fear of what Trouble Later might mean, my hands begin to sweat and my breathing quickens. The pressure in my brain begins to build again, and my vision clouds.

"Well, what are *you* staring at, Mouse Girl?" Melissa asks and takes a step toward me.

And just as I am thinking that Trouble Later means Trouble Now because they're heading toward me, and I can barely stand so fuzzy is my brain, I'm wishing with all my might that Mr. Fenton will NOTICE THEM and GET RID OF THEM, the pressure in my brain vanishes abruptly. He stops flirting with Miss-not-Ms. Ethelridge and NOTICES THEM.

"Everyone to their lessons," Mr. Fenton says, clapping his hands. "Well, girls, what are you waiting for?"

Melissa says something to Bev and smirks slyly at me as they leave. Mr. Fenton hasn't, however, even noticed that I am still here, and I am still clutching the chair, and my head is killing me. But someone else has.

"Hey, are you okay?" Fat Mike asks me, his kind face all concerned. "You looked like you were going to faint or something. You should go and see the school nurse because if you do faint, you could break an arm during the fall or hit your head or something. Then you could get an aneurysm in your brain and even die."

Gee, thanks, Mike.

But I'm definitely not worrying about breaking an arm or cracking my skull or getting brain aneurysms at the moment. I have much bigger fish to fry than that because An Idea has just occurred to me and I do not like it one bit.

I am more concerned that I seem to have developed some weird mental powers. Which is totally, utterly impossible, because it's just not logical, and there must be another explanation.

But then another thought occurs to me.

A not-very-pleasant other thought.

My situation is just like John Travolta's in the movie *Phenomenon* where John plays an ordinary, well, john (who is a mechanic and not a member of MENSA or any other organization related to high IQs), and one day he sees a bright light in the sky and the next day he develops super-intelligence and telekinesis, and then the government wants to get its hands on him so that he can do, you know, mind stuff to the bad guys, and he will be a prisoner for the rest of his life because they are all afraid of him. But then he dies because the super-powers are really a *brain tumor*!

I am too young to die of a brain tumor!

Aren't I?

Chapter 3

 OME SYMPTOMS THAT MAY BE CAUSED BY A
POSSIBLE BRAIN TUMOR:

1. Headache. (Check.)
2. Vomiting. (Nausea is almost vomiting. Check.)
3. Uncoordinated, clumsy movements. (Stumbling is certainly clumsy and uncoordinated.)
4. Mental changes. (Developing mind control is definitely a mental change.)

Honestly, you'd think that the school nurse would be more sympathetic (and knowledgeable) about possible brain tumors, wouldn't you?

Then again, you'd think that the school health-care representative would be, oh, in her office during school hours, instead of watching reruns of an old American TV show called *Dallas* in the staff sitting room. At least it gave me a good half hour to surreptitiously check my symptoms on her computer.

When Mrs. Hunter finally arrived, and I told her about the splitting headache and nausea and nearly fainting (but not the part about my newly developed possible mind-control powers) she was all, "It's nothing to worry about, dear, it's normal for girls of your age to get headaches and fuzziness—especially at that time of the month, if you know what I mean."

She's a qualified health-care professional and she calls those symptoms *nothing to worry about*? Even though I told her this isn't my "that time of the month"? This, from the woman who considers finding out who really shot J. R. Ewing (a fictional TV character) more important than helping a student (a real person) in need.

And then she gave me a cookie because she said she knew that "you girls" are all dieting too much these days because of all the underweight supermodels. Even though I explained that no, I hadn't missed breakfast, therefore nearly fainting could not be attributed to lack of food. And did she know about the lack of nutritional value in cookies?

I don't think she appreciated that comment. She just shook her head and told me that she couldn't administer painkillers because the school isn't allowed to do this without parental consent. Which seems rather ironic to me in view of the fact that the school *is* allowed to administer torture in the form of forcing us to wear ugly bottle green skirts, white shirts, burgundy jackets, and burgundy-bottle-green-and-yellow-striped school ties without anyone's consent. I mean, how can anybody look good in these colors?

Then, when I asked to ring home for permission to get an aspirin (!), she gave me her spiel about teenagers these days taking too many unnecessary drugs, and I had to nearly beg to get her to let me make a call. I rang Mum's assistant, Sharon, instead, because I knew that Mum was really busy today, and Sharon always knows what to do in any given situation.

"Sweetheart, yer mum's about to leave the building fer a really important meeting with Madonna. But no worries," she told me in her broad Cockney accent.

Within seconds, she'd patched me through to Mum's mobile phone. I assured her I was fine, really (sometimes it's better to not tell parents the whole truth), just needed some Tylenol, then I handed her over to Mrs. Hunter.

After some back and forth during which Mrs. Hunter questioned whether Mum was really Mum (and during which I furtively took the cookie, because inexplicably I was ravenous), she finally hung up and gave me two pills. Begrudgingly.

All that fuss for two Tylenol! It would've been funny if I hadn't had a splitting headache.

"Where were you for history?" Gina asks me, as I take my place next to her for English class.

"I had a pounding headache, so I had to go see Mrs. Hunter," I tell her, trying to make light of it. Even though my head is still pounding. "You wouldn't believe how hard it was to get my hands on two Tylenol." I wonder if Tylenol even works on possibly brain-tumor-related headaches.

Fortunately nobody paid any attention to me as I came into the room last because most of the thirty kids in my English class have split up into the Cliques and are too busy cliqueing away to notice me.

The Cliques are the same wherever you go.

Clique One: the popular kids and the jocks—Melissa Stevens, Bev Grainger, Suzy Langton, Chaz Peterson (Suzy's boyfriend), and the rest—holding court in the middle of the room and generally lording it over the rest of student kind.

Clique Two: the wannabe popular kids—like Stephanie Gordon and Karen Goodwin—sitting on the fringes of the Clique One kids. I don't know why they bother because as far as I know from Gina, they've been living in hope since grade school.

Clique Three: the troublemakers and loners at the back of the room. Among them: Andrea Spencer, who used to be a Clique One girl until she and Melissa fell out. Nobody knows what about, it's all a bit of a mystery.

Clique Four: the nerds at the front, like Nicholas Bergin, Harry Emond, and the rest of the computer and chess club members, arguing about which is more intellectual, chess or the new killer RPG world conquest game. Or both.

The so-called clique-free losers like Fat Mike and Gaynor Cole sit near the door, so as to make a quick exit when the lesson is over.

And then you have the other clique-free stragglers—Gina and me. We sit *near* the front but not *at* the front, in the fringes of the wannabe popular kids. This is part of the Total Anonymity plan—teachers always pay attention to the troublemakers at the back and ask questions of the nerds at the front. And the troublemakers at the back don't pay us attention because we're hidden among the wannabe popular kids.

"But you were fine this morning. You never have head-aches," Gina points out. "Do you think there's something wrong with you?" Her sweet face is all screwed up with con-cern, and I think, *Why worry her?* She'll have plenty of time later to miss me one way or the other.

"It's probably stress," I say, and my headache is still really bad. "I'll be okay when the Tylenol kicks in." Then I distract her by telling her about Mrs. Hunter, *Dallas*, Mum, and Madonna, and all that fuss about the painkillers.

"Wow. Your mum has a meeting with Madonna? *The* Madonna? That's so, so—"

"Book?" I suggest.

"That's the word! You're really getting the hang of Kieran's slang now. He's so sublime, isn't he?" The way Gina says *Kieran* and *sublime* make me think of Joe and sublime. I also think of who Gina will have to love When I Am Gone.

"Yes, Gina, he really is." Why stomp on her Kieran fantasy? We all have our dreams.

And then we don't talk anymore because Ms. Woods, our English teacher, floats into the room on a cloud of patchouli oil, a long, wilting skirt, and long, wilting hair. Gina and I hunch down in our seats because this helps with Total Anonymity.

"Good morning, class," she trills, beaming hopefully at us all. She is always hopeful that it will be a good morning and that her class won't disintegrate into madness and mayhem because she's not exactly what you might call authoritative. So everyone usually ignores her and carries on with whatever they were doing before she arrived. Today is no different.

"Today, we're going to write a short essay about what we want to do when we leave school," she continues in her optimistic way, even though only about five people in the room are listening to her. "And then we're going to read them aloud."

It must be that time of year again when Ms. Woods wants to "connect" with us on a more personal level.

When we have to do this touchy-feely sharing kind of stuff in Ms. Woods's class it is totally imperative to lie! I mean, who wants to write down that they want to be a famous movie star (instant ridicule unless you are Melissa), or a racing-car driver (more ridicule), or a stock-broker (believe me, this would get more ridicule than the first two options).

"I'm going to write one about being a secretary," I whisper to Gina. "Mum's secretary, Sharon, is really clever, and speaks French and German, and has to deal with all kinds of prob-lems, but when you say 'secretary,' people generally assume that the only things they do are make coffee and type."

"Good choice," she whispers back to me. "How about bank clerk for me?"

"Good solid choice."

"Before we begin," Ms. Woods says, although we can hardly hear her because of the noise volume. "I see we have a new student. Would you like to introduce yourself?"

"Oh," Gina whispers as we see the new girl standing in the doorway. "Oh, dear."

New Girl is a fourteen-year-old Ms. Woods clone!

"Hi, everyone," New Girl says, smiling broadly back at Ms. Woods, and Gina and I roll our eyes at each other. We just know this is going to be bad. Really bad. What kind of crazy parents allow their daughter to wear such a mismatched, ill-fitting uniform? I mean, that skirt is definitely more forest green than bottle green, and is too long, and her jacket is way too big, and her long, mousy hair is just everywhere!

Although Ms. Woods can't command attention from the class, the sight of New Girl is enough to quiet down the whole room. You could hear a pin drop!

What delusional parents make their kid move to a different school during the final few weeks of the summer term? Are they lunatics?

"My name is Peaceflower Moonbeam," she tells us in a softly burring west-country accent, which makes her stick out even more. "I've just moved here from a commune in Wiltshire."

Ah, *those* kind of parents.

Melissa Stevens and Gang are all, *Oh my God, what is she wearing, what a freak,* and giggling, and my head throbs even more at the thought of how Peaceflower Moonbeam is going to suffer them.

"My respected grand elder—that's my mother's mother—can't live on her own anymore so we moved in with her," she continues, and Gina and I roll our eyes even more, as the sniggers and rude comments get louder. Who calls their grandmother their grand elder, by the way?

"Um, it's lovely to be here and I'm looking forward to meeting everyone," she says, faltering a bit as the cliques resume their cliqueing.

Peaceflower Moonbeam obviously has a complete death wish.

Not lying madly about her name was a majorly big mistake. *Huge mistake.* I mean, if my real name were Peaceflower Moonbeam, because my parents were delusional at the time of my birth, then I'd lie and say my name was something normal. Like Anne or Susan. But her Totally Genuine Politeness has sealed her fate.

"We're all pleased to meet you, aren't we, class?" Ms. Woods burbles on, and because my head is still throbbing, and I'm not paying proper attention to Total Anonymity, I should guess what comes next.

"Let's see." Ms. Wood scans the room, and I accidentally make eye contact with her! "Why don't you sit there with Gina and Fiona. Girls, you'll take care of Peaceflower, won't you? Make her feel welcome and show her around the school? Sit with her at lunch, and whatnot?"

We. Are. Doomed.

"So, this is really nice of you," Peaceflower says, as Gina and I try to find a table in the noisy lunchroom. The dynamics in the lunchroom pretty well resemble Ms. Woods's classroom, except instead of thirty kids there are about a hundred in here for early lunch, all cliqueing away as per usual.

Melissa is holding court near the center of the room, and Joe is not with her. Which means that she'll feel free to be nasty to some poor victim. We don't want it to be us, so after exchanging a mutually knowing glance, Gina and I guide Peaceflower to the fringe of the wannabe Clique Two students.

"I thought it would be awful moving schools, because I loved the commune school, but it's not at all, is it? And London is such a big city," Peaceflower chatters on. "I've never lived in a city before. I just didn't know what to expect. But this is great!"

If only she knew the truth, I think, forcing myself to smile despite my headache, which is a bit better due to the pain medication but has not completely gone away.

"How about here?" Gina asks, as we find the perfect solution table. "A can't-see-the-woods-for-the-trees table!"

"Brilliant suggestion," I tell her, keeping an eye on Melissa and Gang. But it's okay because they're preoccupied with a bride magazine. Melissa is definitely looking a bit too far into the future, I think, as a horrible image of her in a marshmallow dress and Joe all handsome in his morning suit pops into my mind before I can stop it. They are standing at an altar and are about to take their vows!

"Is that some kind of code?" Peaceflower is baffled, and I quash the horrible Joe/Melissa image.

"Don't worry," I tell her. "You'll get used to us. Gina just meant that this would be a great table for us."

"Oh." She accepts my explanation without comment and she's back in happy mode in a heartbeat. "I'm just so thrilled I made two friends on my first day!" Peaceflower squeaks, and I feel instantly horrible because I really don't want to be here with her. But she is so friendly and naïve, which makes me feel even *more* mean and cowardly. Like I've kicked a puppy!

"Well, we're very glad to have you here, aren't we, Gina?" I nudge Gina, who is distracted by the sight of Kieran three tables away.

"Oh yes, yes, we are, it's totally buzzing," Gina tells her.

"Buzzing?"

"Don't worry about her," I say to Peaceflower. "Buzzing is, apparently, the new 'cool.' Well, another new version. There are just so many," I say, rolling my eyes at Gina. Which makes my eyeballs hurt, so I wince.

"Is that code, too?" Peaceflower squints as she thinks about it. Then she surprises me. "You know, you should come down to Portobello Road and check out my elders'—that's my parents—health store," Peaceflower says fairly loudly, oblivious to the odd glances she's receiving.

Okay. I should not be surprised that a girl who calls her grandmother her *grand elder* and her parents her *elders* is into alternative medicine. But really, Peaceflower needs to stop being so visible.

"Um, I'll be sure to check it out," I say, a bit halfheartedly, as I open my lunchbox and take out a tuna sandwich. All of a sudden I'm desperately ravenous, despite my head.

"Because I noticed that you winced just now, which indicates pain, and Pansy, that's my mother by the way, is great with alternative pain management. Crystals are very popular."

And I thought Peaceflower was unobservant.

"So, tell me about yourselves." Peaceflower is oblivious to the odd looks she's getting from the surrounding tables as she loads her fork with the strange-looking salad in her lunchbox. "How long have you been friends? It's good to have friends—that was the hardest thing about leaving the commune. Oh, and leaving my boyfriend, Carl. We've known each other forever," she tells us. "But we'll see each other during the holidays, and there's always e-mail, isn't there? Oh, do you want to see a photo of him? I have one in my bag somewhere."

In a moment of totally terrible timing, before Gina or I can stop her, Peaceflower stands up, smooths down her too-long skirt, and hoists her big, orange, flower-covered backpack onto the table. If that isn't bad enough, she knocks it over, and the backpack topples to the floor. Its contents scatter loudly all over the lunchroom floor. I drop my half-eaten tuna sandwich into my lunchbox, and Gina and I look at each other across the table. Our cover is blown.

The students at the surrounding tables snigger, and some comment on Peaceflower's odd appearance. They're all, "Nice one, hippie girl, what do you do for an encore?" and making horrible comments about Peaceflower's clothes. And I can see that Peaceflower is upset because her pixie face is all scrunched up.

"Don't pay attention to them," I tell her. "Come on, let's get your stuff together."

Gina and I scramble to the floor to help her retrieve her belongings, and just as I pick up one of her books titled *Love and Peace: Karmic Bliss,* I get tingles at the back of my neck. I glance up, and there, in front of me, are three pairs of female legs. No Karmic bliss for us.

"Oh, dear, what a shame." Melissa is all faux sympathy. "But you know, you don't have to bow to me."

Bev and Suzy snigger, and I feel my face go red as I try to ignore them and concentrate on Peaceflower's stuff.

"But what a *lovely* backpack," Melissa says. "What a shame you're so clumsy because it's too *beautiful* to fall on the floor, don't you think, girls?"

"I've never seen one like it before," Bev gushes insincerely and—I can't help it—it makes me so mad that the tingles at the back of my neck turn into a huge prickle. I stand up.

"Didn't they used to be popular, like back in the sixties? All that flower power?" Suzy looks at Melissa and Bev, and the condescension on their faces makes me want to scream.

"Yes." Peaceflower smiles gratefully up at them because she doesn't realize that they are poking fun at her. "Pansy, that's my mother, got it from a thrift store in Glastonbury."

"Oh, it must be lovely to be such a fashion guru." Melissa rolls her eyes and laughs insincerely.

Why are these people so horrible? I mean, Melissa has Joe Summers. You'd think that she'd be one of the happiest people alive, so why poke fun at Peaceflower?

It's so unfair, because all we want to do is eat our lunch in peace. We're nice, inoffensive people who just, you know, want to survive school relatively unscathed, and what did we ever do to anyone, by the way? And now I'm really furious because this is just so wrong.

As I get even angrier, my headache returns with full force along with the pressure in my brain. It's really pounding, and I'm thinking, GO AWAY and LEAVE us ALONE. I'm really wishing with all my heart that they'd FORGET ABOUT US AND LEAVE.

I start to see black spots in front of my eyes and I can barely hold up my head. And just when I think my head is going to explode, the pressure vanishes.

"Only the best people shop in thrift—" Melissa stops mid-sentence, and all three of them look at one another in puzzlement, as if they can't remember why they're here. "Where was I? Oh, I really love Vera Wang's latest bridal collection," Melissa says to Bev and Suzy.

"You're such a Vera kind of girl," Suzy tells her as they turn to leave.

"But Stella McCartney is so—so twenty-first century, too," Bev adds.

I slump down in my seat.

"What just happened there?" Gina asks me, shaking her head as she watches them walk away. "That was, like, totally weird but I'm not complaining. I thought we were going to be verbal toast."

"Um, mass amnesia?" I say feebly.

I can't ignore it. This is obviously a sign that I really do have some sort of mind-control power, which is totally mad. I feel nauseous, so I close my eyes. For a moment I feel like I might be sliding off my seat. I'm going to pass out. I'm really going to pass out in the middle of the lunchroom.

"Fiona, you're all white. This is getting scary." Gina's voice comes from a long way away, but I can hear the worry in her tone, as she props me up. "We should get you to the nurse's office."

"You really don't look well," Peaceflower tells me as she selflessly abandons the rest of her strewn belongings to take my other arm. "Is it that time of month? Some women get faint and nauseous at that time of month."

Then someone else arrives on the scene.

"Hey, girls, what's going on? Are you okay, Fiona?" Joe Summers asks me, and I open my eyes.

Great, just what I need.

Joe Summers as a witness to me either (a) barfing, (b) fainting, or (c) quite possibly both.

This day just gets better and better!

According to findyouronetruelove.com, the current "book" place (so says Gina) to go on the Internet for relationship advice, here are some hot tips on how to respond during a chance meeting with your One True Love.

1. Smile and say, "Hello."
2. Introduce a topic of conversation that you know will be of interest to the object of your desire.
3. Listen to what he says with interest.
4. Laugh at his jokes.

Nowhere does it say you should:

1. Mumble, "Hmffph," in an I-am-an-idiot-I-can-barely-put-two-words-together kind of way, thereby giving him the impression that you are, in fact, a total idiot who cannot put two words together.
2. Put a hand to your mouth, hold on to your stomach (which is queasy due to developing weird powers) with the other, and make a quick dash to the nearest bathroom, thereby giving your loved one the impression that the mere sight of him makes you sick.

But that's exactly what I did after Joe spoke to me. I mean, what I really needed today after (a) possibly finding my father, (b) developing weird powers, and (c) discovering a potential brain tumor, was him to think that I'm an idiot!

On the plus side, despite the nausea and nearly fainting, I still managed to make my legs work long enough to get to the bathroom where, inexplicably, I did not throw up.

Also on the plus side, my headache isn't so bad.

Well, they do say that love is the great healer. Or it could be the pain meds kicking in.

Anyway, Joe's probably forgotten all about me now because as I ran out of the lunchroom, I heard Melissa say, "Hi, Joe, where have you been? We saved a place for you," in her sugariest tone of voice, like she hadn't been mean to Peaceflower a few seconds beforehand.

At least she distracted Joe from my humiliation. She has her uses.

But why, oh why, did I have to make such a fool of myself

in front of him? I will never live it down! Not that I'll be alive for very long . . .

"Fiona," Gina says as she and Peaceflower rush into the bathroom after me. "Are you okay? Because I'm really getting swag about you, all this near-fainting and such."

"I'm okay," I tell her as I splash cold water on my face.

"Joe was really worried about you, too," she adds, and I splash even more water over my suddenly hot face. "Melissa was all, 'Oh, and did you see that article I sent to you earlier about investing in that soft-toy company? Aren't those stuffed kitties just the cutest thing you've ever seen?' And then, when he asked us what happened, she was all, 'Poor Fiona,' and faux sympathy. That girl is such a two-faced twit."

"Gina! I think that's the meanest thing I've ever heard you say."

"I thought Melissa was nice." Peaceflower shrugs.

She'll learn.

"She deserves it. After all, Joe was concerned about you, and quite rightly so, because he is the best friend of your best friend's brother, which makes him practically family."

Honestly Gina's logic is beyond comprehension some-times. No way does that make Joe nearly my family because me liking him would be practically incest! I grab the paper towel Gina is holding out to me and bury my red face in it. I have got to stop blushing whenever his name is mentioned.

To hide my embarrassment, I ask her, "What is swag?" I suspect that I have Kieran to thank for it. Plus it effectively changes the subject from Joe.

"Oh, swag means, you know, 'scared' or 'worried,' and I am. Scared and worried. Because what if it means that you're really ill with a *brain tumor* or something?"

Gina's so perceptive! I mean, it's easy to assume that she thinks more about Kieran and being cool than anything else. Her sweet face is clouded with worry, and she gives my arm a supportive squeeze. And it's comforting, it really is nice, to have at least one friend who cares about me.

"Or it could be that your chakras are not synchronized because of your time of month," Peaceflower says. "Pansy's a whiz at straightening out chakras. She does private sessions, if you're interested. She also does group chanting and meditation."

It is really sweet that Peaceflower wants to help me, a person she has only just met.

"Um, thank you," I say, trying not to sound dismissive of alternative medicine, even though it has to be said that I think most of it might be mumbo jumbo. Although I could be wrong. And I definitely think that a bit of peaceful meditation can be helpful.

Then I realize that I have been approaching this from completely the wrong angle!

What would Albert Einstein do?

He wouldn't jump to the brain-tumor-and-special-powers assumptions based on one day's worth of me getting brain-splitting pressure headaches, and buzzing in my ears, and clouded vision, would he? I mean, there must be other explanations, mustn't there?

At that moment I remember what we talked about in science class earlier in the week, and I know what I am going to do.

I am going to apply Occam's razor.

Occam's razor (which is attributed to the fourteenth-century Franciscan friar and person of logic, William of Occam) says that you should first look for the simplest explanation for something. If you have two or more hypotheses that describe exactly the same thing (my symptoms), you should look to the simplest one. You know, you razor off the superfluous bits that you don't really need.

The assumption that I made: that I have some sort of mind-control power and a brain tumor. All day I have been making the facts fit the assumption, instead of examining the facts and coming to a logical conclusion, as per William of Occam's advice. I mean, my symptoms could be caused by a lot of other, much simpler things, too, which have exactly the same symptoms as a brain tumor (but not the mind-control symptoms).

Headaches, nausea, fainting . . . I mean, for all I know they could simply be the result of something I ate last night. Thinking of food makes me ravenous again, which is odd because how can I feel ravenous and nauseous at the same time?

"I have something that will help," Peaceflower tells me as she rummages in her backpack. "Yes! Here it is. Now, I know we've only known each other for an hour or so, but I feel like I've known you both for ages and I want you to take this." She presses a clear crystal into my hand and folds my fingers around it. "This is my special crystal. All you have to do is focus on your pain and nausea and concentrate on the crystal. Imagine the crystal is absorbing all that pain, and you should feel a lot better really soon," she says solemnly. "It always works for me."

"That's really good of you," I say, touched by her concern and already feeling less stressed now that I know how to proceed. "But you know—I'm feeling a bit better now."

"That's because the crystal is already working," she tells me earnestly, still clutching my hand. "But you can keep it in your pocket out of sight if that's what's worrying you. People can be quite rude about crystal therapy, you know?"

"Um. Thank you." How nice is that! How can I say no?

I obviously need to do more research and observe myself more (and write a will, just in case). Also, I need to test the William Brown Talking Head on Gina (as part of the brain-tumor research).

So much to do, so (possibly) little time.

Chapter 4

ERSONAL STUFF I KNOW ABOUT MUM'S WB

The basics:

Age: 37
Hair color: brown
Eyes: brown
Height: about six feet
Build: well-built but not fat

Other stuff:

- He is American (Mum says he'd just finished his bachelor's degree in math in New Jersey, but she can't remember which state he was actually from).
- He loves (used to love) skiing, reading, traveling (obviously), and music (also obviously), with a particular fondness for lots of old bands/artists like Bruce Springsteen, U2, and David Bowie. And Elvis (who is timeless).

- When he was fifteen, his black Labrador named Pixel died.
- He doesn't get along with his parents (much like Mum used to be with Grandmother).
- He was planning to be a math teacher on account of wanting to work with kids.

I cannot go home with Gina today, which means I cannot test the William Brown Talking Head thing on her right away because there is something that I have forgotten.

"It's just not good enough, Fiona," Grandmother Elizabeth lectures me on the phone, which I made the mistake of picking up because I was distracted with the William Brown list, instead of letting it go through to voice mail. "You are a de Plessi and de Plessis are achievers. Most of them, at any rate," Grandmother Elizabeth adds. Then she sniffs. Whenever she does that, I immediately conjure a picture of her sitting on a throne, complete with gloves, handbag, and tiara.

"Yes, Grandmother Elizabeth," I say very solemnly because it's best to keep conversations with her as brief as possible.

"Lady Burleigh's granddaughters attend Bunting Hall. Very reputable school. Very suitable for families such as ours. If only your mother hadn't run off to be a musician, you would be taking your proper place there with all the other young ladies."

"Yes, Grandmother Elizabeth," I say, tuning her out, because I know this lecture by heart and therefore can concentrate on other things.

What I have forgotten is that getting my report card also means that tonight is parent-slash-teacher-slash-student appointments at school, where my homeroom teacher, my parent, and I communicate with one another about my grades (the teacher and Mum communicate—I try not to say very much).

I fear that this forgetfulness is another symptom of my possible brain tumor.

"So, I've reserved a place for you to commence in the autumn term. It's all arranged."

"What?" I say before I can stop myself.

"'Pardon,' not 'what,'" Grandmother Elizabeth corrects me. "'What' is so common."

"Sorry, Grandmother Elizabeth." Bunting Hall? I'll let Mum sort that one out later. She's much better at dealing with Grandmother Elizabeth than I am. "Um, I have to go now. To get ready for parent-slash-teacher-slash-student night."

I think Mum's forgotten about it, too. It's seven-thirty and the appointment is for eight-fifteen. It's hardly surprising since she had so much to tell me this morning. Plus the Madonna meeting. But what is the point of even going? I mean, I got straight Bs on my report card except for one A. Same as last term. End of story.

"I beg your pardon? What on earth kind of mumbo jumbo is that?" Grandmother Elizabeth booms, as Mum comes in through the front door. I smile and hold my fingers to my lips, so she knows who I'm talking to. It's code. Because Grandmother Elizabeth will insist on talking to Mum if she knows she's here.

"Sorry, Grandmother Elizabeth, it's a school thing," I say as I slip the William Brown list back into a folder. "I really have to go and get ready."

"Hmph. Well, I expect you'd better go, then. I'll speak with you more about Bunting Hall later, you can be sure of that." And she hangs up without even saying good-bye. For someone who places such importance on good manners, she can be very rude!

"I come bearing takeout," Mum says, holding up a bag of Chinese food. "All the quicker to eat and get to the school."

"I thought you'd forgotten."

"I did, but I have Sharon to remind me," Mum says as she gets plates out of the cupboard and takes two cartons out of the bag. "Everyone could do with a Sharon. General Tso's for two. Make that three," she adds as Daphne Kat rubs herself around Mum's ankles.

"I don't think General Tso's is on the list of dietary requirements for cats," I say. "I don't think it's on the human dietary requirements list, either."

"Let your hair down, Fiona, live a little." Mum laughs and hugs me. "Now come and eat, and tell me about your day. Is your head feeling better?"

"I'm fine. And nothing much to tell. Same old, same old," I say (which is not a lie but not the whole truth), and I fork a piece of chicken into my mouth. Hmm, delicious! I shouldn't really be hungry because when I got home from school I had a grilled cheese sandwich and a banana, but I'm starving! I know General Tso's is bad for my arteries, but Mum has a point about living a little. Because I might not be around that long. Which reminds me . . .

There is a conversation I have with Mum practically every time I (a) start at a new school, (b) begin a new school term, or (c) finish every new school term when I have received a report card. So it would be like breaking tradition if I didn't have it with her now.

ME: [*all reasonable in a grown-up kind of way*] You know, I think I'd get much better grades if I was homeschooled. I'd have no distractions, I'd get tons more work done, and I think it would dramatically improve my concentration.

MUM: [*laughing*] Not this old dead horse again.

ME: [*still reasonably*] See, I would be so focused you wouldn't believe it, and I'm really self-motivated. I bet I'd get straight As for everything.

MUM: [*still laughing*] No.

ME: And, you know, it would mean that I'd get better schooling in general, on account of not having thirty other students in the same classes. Plus it would save you money because you wouldn't have to buy me expensive school clothes. And it wouldn't interfere with your career at all because I'd have the Internet and textbooks and I could homeschool me myself.

MUM: [*unwavering in her resolve*] As I have said many times, I still don't think it's a good idea.

I think it's a perfectly sound argument. I would avoid Mean Melissa and Gang, school in general, plus I wouldn't have to worry about not getting straight As. A win-win situation. Of course, I'd miss Gina. But it would give her time to get used to the idea of me not being around (just in case). Not seeing Joe every day would be a great hardship, too.

As we walk to school for our meeting, I cunningly bring the subject back around to me homeschooling myself.

MUM: [*who still insists on laughing*] Fiona, school isn't just about grades. It's also about teamwork and making friends and Getting On With Society as a Whole. Besides, if you really wanted to get straight As you could do it in school.

ME: [*with a new strategy*] Why don't we compromise and try it just for one term? Then, if it doesn't work out, I'll go back to regular school.

MUM: [*quite serious*] Dear Fiona, I worry that you spend too much time alone as it is. I think it's my fault for having moved you around so much. Do you really hate school that much?

And then, as I do tonight, I usually cave in, because I don't want to worry her. She looks so sad for me because I am not sociable like her, and I only have one friend. *One friend is fine by me,* I want to say, but don't, because Mum gets on with everyone and cannot understand why I do not. I think her relationship with Grandmother Elizabeth also makes her worry about her relationship with me.

I wish, sometimes, that Mum would meet a man and start dating because that might lighten her up a bit. Plus, she deserves to find someone who is nice and kind to her (and would be a companion for her in the event that I am not around for much longer).

ME: No, I don't hate it. [*with a sigh*] I just don't feel as if I belong, that's all.

MUM: It just takes time, dear, that's all. You have to make more of an effort to get on with people and make friends. Will you try? For me?

ME: [*with another sigh*] Yes. I will try.

(But I have been at this school for three years already. How much more time does it take?)

"By the way," I ask Mum as we reach the school gates. "How was Madonna?"

"She sends her love," Mum says with a straight face, not missing a beat. And then we both burst out laughing because, of course, I've never met her. It feels good to laugh after all the worries of the day.

I stop laughing when we go through the school gates, though, because I get the familiar prickle at the back of my neck. Melissa and her parents are heading toward us! I needn't worry about being noticed, though, because Melissa's too engrossed in arguing with her parents.

"I think it's mean of you to cancel my Manhattan trip," Melissa tells her father petulantly as they get nearer. "It was only two itty-bitty Bs, after all. Tell him, Mum!"

"John, she's right. The trip to Manhattan would be so culturally enlightening for her. And for me." Melissa's mother is the spitting (yet older) image of Melissa. "It's unreasonable to deny her that trip."

"Unreasonable? After all that money I donated for the gymnasium, I expect results," her dad says firmly. "Straight As or no trip."

"But. It's. Just. Not. Fair. You. Promised!" Melissa bursts into tears, but I suspect they are fake, just like the rest of her.

"I'm not backing down this time," Mr. Stevens says firmly and rolls his eyes at Mum as we pass. "If you spent less time playing at that dating site or running up my credit cards, we wouldn't be having this conversation."

"I hate you, *Daddy*."

"There, there, dear," we hear Melissa's mother say. "What about that nice cashmere sweater we saw in Harrods? That'll make you feel better, despite nasty Daddy."

"Helen, can't you see that you're only making things worse? Your daughter is turning into a prima donna who expects everyone to give in to her every demand."

"Friend of yours?" Mum asks as we walk up the steps and into the school.

"No." Definitely not.

"Er, Ms. Blount!" Mr. Fenton jumps out of his chair as Mum and I enter the classroom. "A delight to see you, as usual. A delight," he says, practically leaping across the room. He wipes his palm on his trousers before offering his hand to Mum. She has this effect on people. Well, on men.

"How's it going, Mr. Fenton?" Mum grins as she shakes his hand. "Haven't the students driven you insane yet?"

"Er, er, yes!" He laughs in a peculiarly wheezy kind of way. "I mean, no, no, not your Fiona. Never Fiona. Very charming student. Very hard worker."

Poor Miss Ethelridge! If only she could see the love of her life melting into a puddle in the presence of Mum. This happens when you have a mother who could be Julia Roberts's twin.

After Mr. Fenton's settled down and flirted with Mum a bit more (or tried to), and we have gone through the whole Fiona-could-do-better spiel and the Fiona-needs-to-be-more-active-in-class spiel, Mr. Fenton tells us all about a new initiative invented by Principal Darnell to torture high school kids.

"This term we're introducing the Social and Charitable

Scheme," Mr. Fenton says almost apologetically. "SACS for short. Each student has to do something Sociable and/or Charitable to gain SACS points and must earn a minimum of fifty points during each term. Er, it doesn't count toward their final score, of course," he adds. "We can't *force* our students to take part in extracurricular activities, but we do, er, strongly encourage them."

"I think this is a wonderful idea," says Mum enthusiastically.

"You do?" Mr. Fenton seems almost shocked.

"Absolutely. Why wouldn't I?"

"It's just that some parents felt that it was, er . . ." He trails off. And I wonder if he means Melissa and her mother when he says this. "Never mind. Er, there are all sorts of things for our students to get involved with, from participating in the drama club to helping out in the community. Here's a list of the types of activities along with the points awarded for each task."

"This is fabulous," Mum says as she reads through the list. "There are things on here that I think you'd enjoy, Fiona. How about Theoretical Stockbroker club?"

I'm not much of a joiner, so on principle I'm against this, but . . . Joe Summers is president of the Theoretical Stockbroker club! If I'm going to be forced into being sociable and/or charitable, I suppose seeing Joe on a regular basis is a small price to pay. Even if it means enduring Melissa.

"Well," I begin.

"Fiona's very interested in the stock market," Mum tells Mr. Fenton, and I mentally thank her. "This would be ideal for her." Yes! Yes it would!

"Marvelous." Mr. Fenton beams. "I'll let Joe Summers know to expect you, Fiona. Also, I think Fiona would be perfect for Mentoring Minds," Mr. Fenton says, turning back to Mum. "It's twice a week after school. Fiona would be assigned a student and would work with them to help them raise their grades. It would help her raise her own grades, too."

Joe takes part in that, too! (Not that I'm a stalker. I'm simply observant.)

"Excellent idea," says Mum. "Where does she sign up for that?"

"First meeting's tomorrow. I'll make sure Ms. Maldine assigns her a partner."

As Mr. Fenton writes down the result of our conversation, I have two thoughts in my mind. If I really do have a brain tumor and my life really is over, (a) I might as well spend as much of it with Joe as possible (even though He Will Never Know Why). Which leads to the other thought, (b) What about possible boyfriends for Mum? And a little voice at the back of my mind says, *What about William Brown?*

I am going to apply Occam's razor to William Brown to see if he is that someone nice who will be good to her.

Action List

1. IM Gina about Funktech (because time might be of the essence, and I can't wait until Gina and I are both together in the same room at the same time with the Internet).
2. Research Funktech (but do not click on Meet Our CEO until feedback from Gina received).

3. Covertly explore Mum's current feelings about her WB before coming to a decision about contacting this WB.
4. Figure out how to contact WB without having to tell him my real reasons (his potential long-lost love and his daughter).

So much to do. It makes me exhausted just thinking about it!

> **TtlAnonymity:** Hi? Gina? Are you there?
>
> <
>
> **Feminista:** Hi ☺! U feeling better? How did yr appointment go?
>
> <
>
> **TtlAnonymity:** I'm ok. I have to join Theoretical Stockbroker and Mentoring Minds.
>
> <
>
> **Feminista:** But u don't need to be mentored! U could get straight As if u wanted. That's crazy!

I love Gina, I really do—she's such a loyal friend, but sometimes . . .

> **TtlAnonymity:** No, I'm the one doing the mentoring.
>
> <
>
> **Feminista:** Oh. I see. Actually I don't mind doing SACS. I'm going to visit elderly people at Granddad's sheltered accommodation. And I'm going to volunteer at the animal hospital.
>
> <

TtlAnonymity: You already do those things! But if visiting with your granddad and his buddies and beating them at poker once a week and helping your dad out at his animal hospital count for SACS, go you!

<

Feminista: It's minty, don't u think? I get to earn points and gain experience of my possible future jobs at the same time! Not sure about being a vet like Dad, tho, because you have to be really smart at science like my brothers. Now poker, I know where I am with that. Oh, Kieran's just put up a new entry on his site. BRB!

<

TtlAnonymity: You're good at other stuff. Three potential vets in the family is more than enough.

<

Feminista: OMG. K's going to be an editor of the school paper for his SACS points.

<

TtlAnonymity: We have a school paper?

<

Feminista: Oh, Fiona. Yes. It's a weekly paper, and it's got short stories, poetry, and a horoscope, as well as school news. And K's going to work on it. How book is that?

<

TtlAnonymity: Totally book ☺. And it's a sign! You're inquisitive and you like to write. Maybe you should join the paper, too, and you could submit ideas for articles to him!

This will give Gina less time to miss me when I am gone!

Feminista: Really? U think?

<

TtlAnonymity: Absolutely. You'd be great. Look, can you do something for me? Can you go to this URL www.funktech.com and click the Meet Our CEO button?

<

Feminista: Okay. BRB.

<

Feminista: I have it on screen. Why am I doing this?

<

TtlAnonymity: You're sure? Do you have a picture of the CEO on your screen?

<

Feminista: Yes. He looks nice. But why am I doing this?

<

TtlAnonymity: Did anything, you know, weird happen when you loaded his picture?

<

Feminista: What do u mean by weird? It's got a lot of cool graphics. Is that what u mean? OMG, I just realized why u told me to go here!!!!! It's yr way of showing me that you've found yr missing link! William Brown! Is this *your* William Brown? Do u think this is yr dad?

She obviously can't see William Brown Talking Head

because she would have said something about it.

TtlAnonymity: Don't know—I only found the website this morning. Haven't told Mum because I wouldn't want to give her false hope. Haven't told anybody but you, and you have to promise to keep it secret.

<

Feminista: It would be totally minty if he turned out to be yr dad!!! He looks nice!!! And handsome. U kind of look like him. And this would totally explain yr headaches and stuff today—I mean, after a shock like finding yr dad after 14 years, anybody would feel ill and off-kilter. What are u going to do about it?

<

TtlAnonymity: You really think I look like him? And I don't know what I'm going to do. I have to think about it some more. Because even if he is my William Brown, he might not be thrilled to discover that he has a long-lost daughter.

<

Feminista: If I had a secret daughter I would be very happy if she came looking for me ☺. I'll help u think it through. Oh, gotta go. Brian wants me off-line so he can install the new router.

I do not point out to Gina that there is no way she could have a secret daughter. But she is sweet to want to help me.

TtlAnonymity: Thank you. But remember—YOU CANNOT TELL A SOUL ABOUT WILLIAM BROWN!!!

<

Feminista: U don't have to shout. I am a Master of Discretion.

<

TtlAnonymity: Sorry!

<

Feminista: No worries ☺ ☺.

After Gina logs off I think of all my symptoms, apply the Occam's razor logic, and come up with this list of possible prognoses:

1. Eye problems.
2. Teeth problems.
3. Ear infection.
4. Hormonal changes due to my age.
5. Migraines.
6. Brain tumors.
7. Superpowers.

It can't be symptom 1 or 2, because I've had recent check-ups. And I don't think I have 3 because my ears feel just fine (except for when I get that buzzing roar like I did earlier today). It could be 5 due to 4, but I first got my periods last year, so I think it would be more logical if I'd gotten 4 and 5 last year.

I've saved the worst and the most outrageous until last.

Obviously I don't want it to be a brain tumor. But super-powers? Like Superman or Spider-Man? In human form, they were shy and unassuming, just like me. But they were orphans, and although I come from a single-parent family, it isn't quite the same.

"What do you think?" I ask Albert on my wall. It's a rhetorical question because I know what he would do. He would be brave and go to the Funktech site again, no matter what. Because it all seems to be related—the mind-control stuff never happened before the William Brown Talking Head. So I type in the URL, and I get instant prickles at the back of my neck as the page begins to load.

I take a deep breath and click the Meet Our CEO button.

William Brown's photo appears on my screen.

Then William Brown Talking Head pops out of my computer screen, and he's in my room. I can barely breathe!

"Don't be afraid," William Brown tells me for the second time today.

I don't click X and shut down my computer this time.

Even though I am now very, very afraid.

"Don't be alarmed, friend. You are special, which is why only you can see this message. Try not to react if there are others in the room with you." I'm thinking, fat chance of not being alarmed. I'm shaking like a leaf! So it's a good job that I am alone!

"By now you've realized that you possess some special gifts that others don't. If anyone else is around, go ahead and close down this window"—William Brown smiles reassuringly—"but please come back later when you're alone so you can hear my entire message."

William Brown pauses for what feels like ten million years, but is in reality about ten seconds, as I am sitting here with my mouth wide-open. I don't feel reassured at all, despite his nice, deep voice and kind, twinkly eyes.

"You've probably been surprised and possibly upset by your developing powers," he continues. I'm thinking that's an understatement. "You may have found yourself in an emotional situation and somehow you've done something that is inexplicable, unbelievable."

Yes, and yes, I think. This whole situation is pretty unbelievable.

"I want to tell you that you're not alone. Many of us have developed powers of Extra Sensory Perception, better known as ESP, a multitude of powers that vary from person to person. Over the years we've reached out secretly to support and help one another, and have discovered how to explore and control our powers. We want to welcome you among us, friend."

Can someone pinch me? I can't believe I'm hearing this. There are more people out there like me?

"It's important that you learn to use your powers wisely for the safety of others and yourself. It's also imperative that you don't tell anyone else about what you're experiencing—that could cause danger to you. But you will not be alone and afraid any longer." Then William Brown gives a phone number and an e-mail address where he can be reached. He pauses, smiles again, and says. "Please get in touch. Good-bye for now, my friend."

Then his talking head vanishes back into the screen.

I click X, turn off my laptop, and try to take in what's just happened.

As I sit motionless in front of my blank screen, all I can think is, at least I don't have a brain tumor.

Chapter 5

Daphne Kat can sense my ESP!

Obviously after watching William Brown Talking Head I couldn't sleep. I had all these thoughts going through my mind like, *I have ESP,* and *there are more people like me,* and *this is more proof that this William Brown is my father because I must have inherited these powers from somebody.* Thoughts like, *I wonder what he means by danger?* Like the government finding out about someone's powers and holding them captive, as per poor John Travolta in *Phenomenon?*

Daphne Kat seemed to know that I was upset because when it got to 3:06:44 a.m. on my alarm clock, I heard her meow and scratch my bedroom door. This was odd, because she usually spends her nights madly chasing pens and various other small things around the living room floor. (I know this because we have hardwood floors and I sleep directly above the living room. I have learned to keep my pens away from Daphne Kat.)

When I let Daphne Kat in, she gave me this strange evaluating stare as if she were trying to communicate with me telepathically. Then she stalked across the room and jumped up on my bed. When I got back in, she snuggled her calico-cat self against my stomach. I don't know if it was part of her cat empathy, but I felt a bit better.

Oh, I don't know what to do. I don't know what to think! I mean, just because William Brown looks nice, and sounds nice, what if his organization is some government agency that will kidnap me and keep me for testing? Or a nefarious ESP organization that's trying to take over the world? Or if I call or e-mail, he'll track me down and I may get whisked away from Mum forever to do ESP stuff for him.

Thank goodness Thursday's almost over. I survived a day at school without incident (except I might have willed Mr. Fenton to stop asking me about Mum). Now I have my first Mentoring Minds meeting to endure. The weekend can't come fast enough. I need some time away from everything to figure out what I'm going to do about all of this. No Melissa and Gang, and no Peaceflower, either.

I don't mean "no Peaceflower" in a bad kind of way—she's a nice girl—but I need to regroup my energies and Peaceflower is high on my energy usage. See, because Gina and I are the only people Peaceflower knows so far, she wants to talk to us by the lockers and sit next to us in lessons. Then she spends lunch with us and chatters on about her boyfriend, Carl, and asks us questions about ourselves. Which is sweet of her, I suppose, but not so good for Total Anonymity. It's like having a trouble magnet attached to us!

Fortunately Melissa and Gang were nowhere to be seen in the lunchroom. The school rumor mill, which would be Clique Two—I overheard them during fifth period—has it that Melissa, Suzy, and Bev were too busy letting air out of certain teachers' tires after a less-than-satisfactory teacher-slash-parent-slash-student meeting last night.

Also, it's impossible to talk about private things when Peaceflower's always around us. Like this morning when Gina and I were having a private conversation by our lockers.

"So last night I did some vital research for you on that person who might be your secret you-know-who," Gina told me, and handed me a beige folder. "To thank you for supporting me in My Love for Kieran."

If only I could tell her what I was doing last night! Just then Peaceflower came running over. "Did the crystal help your migraine?" she asked anxiously. I felt instantly guilty about my mean thoughts, so I told her yes and dug it out of my pocket to give back to her. She was all solemn when she said, "I want you to keep it, in case of future headaches and nausea." Which made me feel even more guilty.

I'm just so confused! As I head toward the library later, thankfully by myself, I think about William Brown, and ESP, and the disappointed look on Peaceflower's face when she asked Gina and me to come home with her this afternoon. Obviously we can't: I'm off to discover who my mentee might be and Gina has the school newspaper meeting. Peaceflower's just joined the school, so she didn't have a teacher-slash-parent-slash-student meeting last night to discuss what she's going to do for SACS points. I think she felt pretty left out. It was written all over her face.

When I push open the library door, I'm apprehensive about the whole Mentoring Minds thing. But I'm surprised at the number of students. There must be at least fifty or sixty kids sitting around the library at little fold-up desks and stackable chairs with another ten kids by the main desk. Presumably they're waiting for instruction about mentoring, so I guess that's where I should go, too.

My first shock is when I see Melissa Stevens with Fat Mike over by the biography section. There she is, in all her blond-haired glory, listening to whatever Fat Mike is teaching her with his math book. She's smiling at Mike in such a saccharine way, and Fat Mike is blushing again. I wish he'd realize that she's using him. I wonder why she hasn't been paired with Joe?

The biggest shock is when I get to the desk to find out who I am supposed to be mentoring. Ms. Maldine, our overly cheerful and committed physical ed teacher, who thinks that we're all angels, is in charge of Mentoring Minds. I get instant prickles.

"Harry Emond, let's see . . ." Ms. Maldine booms in her loud voice. "You're written down to mentor Suzy Langton in physics but she doesn't seem to be here. Suzy Langton? Suzy Langton? Are you here?"

"She couldn't come, Miss," Bev says, and I nearly faint on the spot as the prickles increase. "She had a preplanned appointment with her hair-care provider."

My headache increases as I worry about the prickles because I can almost predict what's coming next. My stomach sinks into my shoes.

"I see." Ms. Maldine checks Suzy's name on her list. "Now for you, Beverly. Oh yes. D average in math," she says loudly enough for every person in the room to hear. For a moment I kind of feel sorry for Bev because it can't be very good for your self-worth if everyone thinks you're stupid, can it?

"Ah yes, you're with Fiona Blount." Ms. Maldine seals my fate. I can't believe that she's assigned me to Bev of all people! How could she *do* this to me? As I wonder how I am going to get through this in one piece, I am fascinated by Ms. Maldine's hairy lip. "Off you go, find a table, and get cracking, girls." Ms. Maldine loses interest in us as Mr. Simpkins, our Theory of Knowledge and chemistry teacher, comes over to speak with her.

Bev stands there glaring at me. I don't know where to look. But we can't stand here forever.

"I don't believe this," Bev says, shaking her head. "Ms. Maldine, can I get someone else to mentor me?" That would suit me just fine, too.

"No, dear," Ms. Maldine says rather absentmindedly because she's too busy with Mr. Simpkins. "Everyone's been allocated."

"But—"

"No buts, dear. Now run along and find a table."

Bev tuts, tosses her hair, and strides off toward Melissa. What can I do except follow her? Will I have to sit near Melissa? Oh, the torture of it! But on the plus side there are no vacant places in the biography section. Bev sighs with frustration and heads to the modern fiction section, instead. Also on the plus side, Joe is mentoring Gina's Kieran only a few desks away, but I don't think he even notices me because he's too busy mentoring. He's explaining to Kieran that DNA is a nucleic acid that contains genetic instructions and so on, and Kieran's agreeing because he gets that part, but when Joe goes on about DNA's information being synthesized by enzymes called RNA polymerases, Kieran's shaking his head. I think Joe needs to simplify his explanations. . . .

I take a seat next to Bev, but she's not saying anything, she's just glowering at the floor. Well, it's not like I'm any happier with the situation.

"Um, which things do you need help with?" I ask Bev finally because we might as well get this torture started and finished. It's not like I can refuse to mentor her, is it? That would give her even more reason to single me out.

"Who are you to mentor me?" Bev spits out, and I nearly fall off my seat because of her fierce expression. Her face is bright red. "You're just some loser girl, another B grade retard, and I'm only here because of the stupid SACS points, get it? It's not like *I'm* stupid, get it? I don't care about math, I just need the stupid points, get it?"

"Um, yes. Okay." I get it.

To keep a low profile, I take out my math homework and pretend to do it because I'm too preoccupied with this bizarre situation. The prickles are still there but not in a fierce way. Covertly I glance sideways at Bev but she's not paying me any attention. She's busy looking through a teen magazine.

Ms. Maldine's booming voice carries across the room (she sounds like Grandmother Elizabeth) as she tells Mr. Simpkins very enthusiastically that she's thinking of getting tickets for the Wimbeldon tennis championship later this month, and what does he think?

I think that she's flirting with him because her face goes all dreamy when she speaks to him. I think that unrequited love is in the air. Gina's love for Kieran and mine for Joe are two examples that spring to mind.

If only you'd wax off your mustache, Ms. Maldine, you might have more of a chance, I think. Then again, Mr. Simpkins is very big and very bushy in the face area so if he kissed her he wouldn't even notice her mustache. Yuck, the thought of them kissing is totally disgusting.

Then I have an idea about testing my ESP. There must be a way I can use it without having to get really upset, or scared, or mad, like I did yesterday. I'm not crazy about the headache and nausea and near fainting, either. If only I could focus!

So I'm going to try to help Ms. Maldine. I try to focus on her and get a tingle at the same time, and I think, *Use a wax strip on your mustache, use a wax strip on your mustache,* over and over again. I concentrate so hard but I can't seem to focus properly. Not even a tiny prickle! Ms. Maldine doesn't stop talking to Mr. Simpkins for a second. No ESP luck.

There was no need to think mentoring would be a great way of spending time with Joe, either. He's far too busy tutoring for anything else. Which is not the complete truth because I have caught him glancing over at me a few times. Each time he looked at me I had my hand on Peaceflower's crystal. . . . Maybe the *crystal* is helping me focus my ESP?

I didn't will him to look at me, did I? Oh, this is all so confusing. If I get in touch with William Brown, maybe he'll be able to show me the ropes.

If only I could figure out a way to contact him without, you know, him knowing that I have ESP. I'm not sure I should take him at face value. What if those ESP people are not like the X-Men, working for good, but are bad mutants trying to take over the world or something?

Clearly I need a mentor of my own.

It's Friday, at last. Just physical ed to get through, then I'm free for the weekend and can spend time figuring out everything with no distractions. Physical ed itself is okay because Ms. Maldine is pretty decent, as teachers go. She is committed to young people and exercise. She felt so strongly about the sorry state of sports in schools and young people not getting the right kind of encouragement and support that she gave up a well-paid job as a personal trainer to movie stars for the thankless and much-less-well-paid job that is teaching.

Gina thinks that's minty, and it is. Only problem is that Ms. Maldine (who is still sporting the mustache) thinks that all of us students are intrinsically good, and doesn't have much intuition when it comes to pairing us up. Example: Today, for tennis, she has chosen Peaceflower and Gaynor Cole to play doubles against Melissa and Suzy. *Bad call, Ms. Maldine!*

Melissa has a way with tennis. Which means that she is very good at hitting the ball *at* her opponent, rather than hitting the ball *away* from her opponent to a part of the court where her opponent cannot return the ball, which is the usual way of playing tennis. She has private tennis lessons and knows all of the moves. I know this because she boasts about it often enough. Unfortunately Suzy is good at tennis in the way that Melissa is (but not quite as good because Melissa wouldn't stand for that).

We have four tennis courts in a square block, which means that only sixteen students out of a class of thirty can play doubles at any one time. And because Gina and I played for the first half of the lesson—thank goodness we got Helen Johnson and Belinda Crawford, committed Clique Two girls who don't cause trouble—we are now observing from the sidelines a surefire disaster in the making.

Gina sighs and shakes her head. "This is not going to be pretty."

"I know." Even Peaceflower's tennis gear (white baggy shorts that dangle to her knees) and baggy T-shirt (which is more gray than white) is a disaster. She definitely needs to develop some school smarts if she is going to survive.

"Best foot forward," Ms. Maldine booms encouragingly as Peaceflower (oblivious to the possible trouble that she is facing) serves to Melissa. Peaceflower serves an ace.

"Oh," Gina says, and we look at each other. "That was a surprise."

"Fifteen-love! Great serve, Peaceflower," Ms. Maldine calls unhelpfully. "Keep up the good work." Then she switches her attention to the players in the next court.

"Oh. My. God," Gina says when Peaceflower delivers another great serve, and this time Melissa does return it, only to be thwarted by Peaceflower smashing the ball effortlessly back over the net. "Does she have a death wish?"

"She certainly has a good, strong forehand serve." That's when I get prickles at the back of my neck.

Peaceflower wins the next serve and the set. Suzy serves the next set, and it's pretty much the same as the first. Gaynor Cole doesn't get a look in because Peaceflower's just all over the court defending her position. Everyone not playing is now engrossed in what is sure to become Peaceflower roadkill. Even Ms. Maldine, who's standing on the side of the court with her hands on her hips, is blowing up on her mustache.

Gaynor serves the next set—easy shots that Melissa and Suzy can return. Gaynor is no fool; it's just less trouble to let them win.

It's during the fourth set—the one we've all been waiting for, because it's Melissa's turn to serve—that the real trouble begins. The prickles at the back of my neck become tingles as Melissa's first serve barely misses hitting Peaceflower in the stomach. But Peaceflower's reflexes are really good and she manages to deflect the ball away from herself. I'm fearful for Peaceflower and exasperated with her at the same time. She's so clueless!

When Melissa is poised to serve her second ball, Bev is all, "God, that hippie girl is such a twit," and "What *is* she wearing?" As if her clothes should make a difference in the way people treat her! But it's when she says, "Melissa's so going to slaughter her," and laughs that I get angry. It's not Peaceflower's fault that she's good at tennis. It's not her fault that Melissa is a bully. It's not her fault that I have ESP and a secret father, either.

"God, that girl is such a control freak," Andrea Spencer says to Bev, and I don't think she means Peaceflower. "Get used to the idea that Melissa is not God."

"You're just jealous," Bev tells her. "Because you're not one of us anymore."

"Yeah, right." Andrea shrugs. "Obviously my life can have no purpose."

It's just not right, deliberately trying to hit an opponent with a fast-flying ball because that someone's new and doesn't fit in. I mean, this is only Peaceflower's second day, and after all the moving around I've done I know what it's like to be the odd-girl-out at school.

Melissa's second serve hits Peaceflower on the leg, and Melissa and Suzy high-five as if it were a job well done! I get even more angry. The roaring in my ears gets louder and the rational voice in my mind says, *Oh, no, here we go again*, as the strange pressure builds in my brain.

"Steady on," Ms. Maldine calls out. "Remember, it's not about winning, it's about taking part."

Tell that to Melissa, I think, as she's poised for her third serve.

"I can't bear to watch," Gina says, covering her eyes. "Let me know when it's over."

I barely hear Gina because as Melissa throws the ball in the air and raises her racket, I REALLY WISH that Melissa's feet will GET TANGLED and make her STUMBLE AND SKIN her KNEE on the tennis court, so that she can't play anymore and CAN'T HURT PEACEFLOWER. I can't control myself. I can't keep the pressure in my head.

And then it happens.

The moment the pressure in my brain disappears Melissa's feet really do GET TANGLED, and she STUMBLES AND SKINS HER KNEE on the tennis court.

It's a good job that I'm already sitting down because if I wasn't, I'd fall.

The whole of the tennis group bursts into laughter at the spectacle of Melissa flat out on the court, and Peaceflower is running over to Melissa to help her. I want to cry out, *Don't do it, Peaceflower,* but my head is pounding so hard with a nauseating headache it feels like I am going to burst a blood vessel. I wonder if people's brain's can burst from ESP?

"Did you see that?" Gina says, turning to me, her mouth wide-open. And then, "Are you feeling okay? You've gone very pale again, like you did yesterday before you nearly fainted."

"I think I'm going to be sick," I tell her, and drag myself to my feet.

"Are you all right in there?" Gina calls out anxiously.

"Yes," I say, and open the stall door. "It was a false alarm. I'm okay." If this is the price I have to pay for ESP, I have to wonder if it's worth it.

"I brought you this." Gina holds out a bottle of water and my tote bag with my secret stash of Tylenol. After yesterday's battle with Mrs. Hunter I didn't want to take any chances in case of an ESP moment followed by a raging headache. "Everyone's in the showers, and Ms. Maldine's busy organizing a bandage for Melissa's knee."

"Thank you." I swallow two tablets, and think about what William Brown said about being a danger to myself. Did he mean that the pressure in my brain could cause an aneurysm or something? Then, something else occurs to me. "Is Peaceflower on her own in the showers?"

"Oh. I didn't think about that." Gina puts her hand to her mouth.

"Me either."

The changing and showering part after physical ed is something that we dread. I mean, how barbaric are communal showers? I'm sure that it must count as child abuse. I think that making all us girls strip naked and shower together is probably against our human rights.

Because it's just a fact that some of us have more attractive underwear than others. And some of us have weight issues or lack-of-boob issues, so it's torture to make us strip, don't you think? It degrades us and gives those more attractive individuals the opportunity to lord it over us lesser mortals. It's also a prime opportunity for someone, if they have something against you, to steal your clothes.

"I can't find my clothes." Peaceflower is near to tears when we reach the showers. "I've asked everyone, but nobody's seen them. I left them there. Right on that bench."

"Maybe somebody mistook them for their own?" Mean Melissa says innocently, as she pulls pantyhose on over her bandaged knee, and everyone laughs.

"You think?" Peaceflower is bewildered. "Maybe they'll realize and come back."

"Yes, I'd die for Peaceflower's clothes. They're just so grooooveeeee." Suzy Langton struts her hips as she says this, and there's more laughter.

"Live in hope, hippie girl!"

"But what am I going to do? I can't go home wrapped in a towel."

"Why not? You could set a new fashion trend."

Melissa really makes me sick. What does Joe see in her? I wish I could muster up enough anger to make her do something really humiliating, like running down the corridor naked, but I don't have any energy left.

"Up to your usual tricks?" Andrea Spencer says to Melissa, as she pulls her school bag onto her shoulder. "God, you are so childish."

"What's that supposed to mean?" Melissa is the picture of innocence.

"Try the showers," Andrea tells Peaceflower as she pauses at the door. "Someone probably threw your clothes in there."

"Why would they do something like that?" Peaceflower's really upset now.

"I don't know what you're talking about." Melissa tosses her hair over her shoulder. "Although Andrea seems to know a lot about the situation. Makes you wonder why, doesn't it? Come on, girls," she says to Bev and Suzy. "Let's go."

Gina and I look at each other. "My size, I think?"

"Definitely," Gina says. "I'll stay with Peaceflower."

Gina and I have this system in which one of us undresses while the other holds up a towel, then the undressed one runs to the showers, discards towel, quickly gets washed, retowels up, then runs back and carries out the same function for the one who is guarding the clothes. Trust me, this really cuts down on the worry that someone (you can guess who) might steal our clothes while we are vulnerable. And we both keep spare clothes in our lockers, just in case, so at least we can save Peaceflower's modesty.

I hurry out of the changing room and race down the halls to my locker. As I open it, a voice says right in my ear, "Hey, Fiona." I nearly jump out of my skin with shock—it's Joe Summers! And he's talking to *me*.

What is the use of having ESP if it doesn't give me any warning that Joe Summers is unexpectedly creeping up on me?

"Oh. It's you!" I say, looking up at him. Then I feel really dumb.

"Yeah." He grins, looking down at himself, then back at me. "I'm still me."

"It's just—I thought you were someone else." Dumber! It must be lack of concentration from William Brown Talking Head worry.

"I could pretend to be someone else, if you'd prefer."

Why would I prefer anybody else? Joe is perfect! Could anybody's hair be more cute—all short and golden brown, with the front flicked up? Could anybody's eyes be that perfectly hazel and smattered with little green flecks?

"Oh no," I say. "I prefer you." And then I'm thinking that having a hot face due to embarrassment does not make me a hot girl. Which are the types of girl Joe dates.

But just for a moment the admiring expression on his face makes me feel like a hot girl, and I wonder if this is flirting. If it is, what do I say next?

"Hi, Joe," Melissa Stevens interrupts, and hooks Joe's arm with her own. I'd forgotten about her status in his life for a moment. And her true Hot Girlness. She's got all the usual suspects with her, so of course I don't have to say anything at all. "Did you get my text? We're all going to Starbucks to hang. You should come. It'll be fun. You can kiss my poor knee better, too, I nearly broke my whole leg in tennis because of that crazy new girl."

So much for the flirting fantasy. I should know better.

"Did you hear about Mr. Fenton's car?" Suzy Langton asks.

"It was so, like, minty," Bev breaks in eagerly. "*Someone* let the air out of Mr. Fenton's tires, yesterday." Which makes them all laugh. Except Joe.

"I like Fenton. As teachers go, he's okay. Poor guy."

"Oh, of course it's not funny," Melissa jumps in. "It's just, like, sometimes when you hear bad news, it's reflexive to laugh by mistake. I'd never do anything like that," she adds, the picture of wide-eyed innocence. Yeah, right!

I grab the bag of spare clothes for Peaceflower and close my locker.

Maybe the skinned knee was her karmic payback.

And then Suzy Langton's boyfriend, Chaz, comes over, and he's all "Hey, Joe, my man," as Bev recounts what she heard as she was passing Principal Darnell's office—that a secret informer told him that Andrea Spencer did the dastardly deed—and I turn to go. Peaceflower awaits me.

"Hey, Fiona, wait." It's Joe again, and he's following me. "I never got to talk to you. Mr. Fenton said you were joining Theoretical Stockbroker club?"

I nod.

"So I thought we should exchange e-mail addresses," he says, and my heart is bumping so loudly he must be able to hear it. "Then I can send you our current portfolio and some other information. If you have any questions, I could fill you in. Here's my e-mail and telephone number," he says, handing me a piece of paper. "Just send me an e-mail. Okay?" He smiles again, and my knees go Weak in His Presence.

"Okay," I say, smiling back. I'm quite the conversationalist!

There's this odd little silence as I try to think of something witty to say, and he is probably wondering how to escape this strange girl.

"Joe, we're leaving," Melissa calls, all smiles.

"I'd better go," he says finally as he hitches his bag on his shoulder. "See you later."

"Um, okay."

Really, could I be more pathetic?

When I get back to the shower room it is empty except for Gina and Peaceflower, who is still under the impression that someone "accidentally" threw her clothes into the showers. It is then that I come to a decision. I am going to help Peaceflower!

"Right," I say, handing my spare clothes to Peaceflower. "There's a lot of stuff you need to know if you're going to make it through school. Here beginneth the first lesson on Total Anonymity in the showers."

My ESP is absolutely no use in helping me decide whether or not to call or e-mail William Brown, I think, as Mum and I weave through the hoards of tourists and Saturday shoppers on Oxford Street.

What if William Brown and his team of techies at Funktech really *can* trace private phone numbers and IP addresses back to their owners? I don't want him turning up on our doorstep out of the blue and giving Mum a shock! Or kidnapping me for testing.

On the bright side (if there can be a bright side to having nausea-inducing, splitting-headache-causing ESP), at least William Brown 101 in my file can't be my dad. Not that there's anything *wrong* with having a dad who creates art out of animal dung, of course. And if he had turned out to be my dad (right age, but too short), I would totally have supported him in his art. But euck!

"That baby pink T-shirt and those hipster jeans are so cute on you," Mum says, taking my arm as we reach Bond Street, where the crowds are even thicker. "Such a nice change from the shapeless sweats you normally wear when you're not in school uniform. You have a lovely figure, Fiona. You shouldn't hide it like you do."

"You're biased." I nudge against her and grin, as we round the corner to our favorite Japanese restaurant.

"And right." She nudges me back and pushes open the door. "You're especially adorable in the cargo pants and diamante kitty tank."

This morning, when she said, "Let's do some fun mother/daughter things today," in a bright kind of voice, I thought, *Why not?* What was I going to do? Brood about William Brown and ESP all day? I just want to forget everything that's happened over the last few days. Even though I am not really interested in fashion, a girl needs some parental bonding time. So I let Mum buy me outfits that she thinks make me look cute. I wonder if Joe would like me in them. . . .

It's when we're eating our lunch, and I'm feeling much better about the whole situation, that I get my first shock of the day.

"Fabulous Fiona, I have something to tell you," Mum says in *that* tone of voice. Then she does that thing with her lip, and I steel myself. "It's not that I wanted to mislead you, I wanted to see how things would pan out before I said anything. It's . . . it's just that for the past few Saturday nights I haven't been going out with my friends. Well, I have actually. One friend, in particular. It'sjustthatI'vemetsomeone."

"A man someone?" I squeak, trying to keep my expression even.

Mum laughs. "Yes, a man someone."

"That's great," I tell her. Although I am so shocked that I stop eating and inadvertently poke my chopsticks into my sticky rice. I never even suspected that Mum has a secret boyfriend. "It's about time you started dating, because, you know, you're really young, and you need to find someone nice. I won't be around forever."

"Are you planning on going somewhere anytime soon? Or do you know something I don't?" she teases me.

I can hardly tell her about my ESP and fear of being whisked off to a secret government location, can I? "Of course not. Although I think Grandmother Elizabeth is planning to ship me off to Bunting Hall for the autumn term, but apart from that, no. Did she tell you about it?"

"Oh, in detail. Bunting Hall, the place for all young ladies of quality. I think she's ordering your uniform as we speak," Mum says, laughing. "She's going to be so disappointed. Again."

"Never mind Grandmother Elizabeth now, tell me about your new squeeze," I say. "I want all the details. Well, not all of them. Just the ones appropriate for my youthful ears. Is he nice?"

"He *is* nice," she says, and I can hear the relief in her voice. "His name is Mark Collingridge," she tells me happily as she dips her California roll into soy sauce. "He's an old acquaintance from my Bliss Babe days—you won't remember him—it was about ten years ago when we were in Hamburg, before the Bliss Babes became popular—but he's back in London permanently now." Her voice is so animated and her eyes so bright and excited, I can see that he's more than just a casual boyfriend. "You're really okay with the idea of me dating?"

"Of course," I say, even though I do mind. Just a teeny bit. But that's because I haven't had to share her with anybody before and am just reacting in normal teenage fashion. Plus, what about William Brown?

"Mark's very kind, and caring, and fun," Mum says, deftly chopsticking up a salmon roll. "But he's a bit shy. You'll have the chance to meet him tonight. He's picking me up, and he's popping in to say hello to you."

"Lovely," I say, aiming for cheerful. "Because I need to speak to him about his intentions toward my mother." Then I smile, because for a moment I can see that she thinks I'm being literal. "Lighten up."

"Do I have a curfew, Mother Hen?"

"Miss," our server interrupts. "It's bad luck to leave your chopsticks sticking out of your food," she tells me in a disapproving voice.

Dear server, you might be right, I think, but do not say.

"Ba—ad boys, ba—ad boys," Mum sings in her smoky voice as she gets ready for her date with Mark Collingridge. "Steal your heart, then depart."

"I hope that the lyrics of that Bliss Babes song don't have anything to do with Mark Collingridge," I whisper to Daphne Kat, who is sitting on my desk watching me very seriously, as I lie on my bed worrying about ESP and William Brown. And Mark Collingridge.

I hear a car pull up outside at 7:29:03 p.m. and I suspect that it must be Mark Collingridge, because Mum said that he would be here at 7:30:00 p.m.

"Destruction boys, destructor toys," Mum belts out over the sound of her hair dryer.

"What do you think?" I ask Daphne Kat. She loses interest in me because my pen is obviously more interesting than my silly concerns about Mum having a boyfriend. "Thanks for your input," I tell her, but she's in serious pen-to-paw-to-other-paw mode now. Some help she is! I mean, I *want* Mum to have a boyfriend. I don't want her to be lonely if something happens to me, but I've always hoped that it might be her William Brown. Our William Brown.

"Fiona, can you get that?" Mum shouts from her bedroom, when the doorbell rings at 7:29:33 p.m. "I haven't done my face yet and I don't want to frighten off Mark," she adds. "I'll be down in a few minutes."

"I don't know why you're worried, you look great without makeup," I call to her as I walk down the stairs. At least Mark Collingridge is punctual, which is a good sign. Then I open the door.

Mark Collingridge is a bit of a shock—he's a hippie in a suit!

"Hello, good God, little Fiona? You won't remember me, you were only about four when I last saw you. I'm Mark." He grins warmly and offers me his hand.

Tall and slim, with long brown hair pulled back in a ponytail. And craggy, rather than handsome, but he has a big smile. He reminds me of an overgrown, exuberant puppy.

"I'm pleased to, um, re-meet you," I say as he pumps my hand vigorously. "Please come in. Mum will only be a few minutes."

"You look ever so much like your mum, it's amazing,"

Mark Collingridge tells me as he follows me down the hall to the living room. I do? I have Mum's long brown hair and brown eyes, but Mum's a babe. "I bet people say that to you all the time. I could see the resemblance the instant you opened the door. And what a lovely room," he chats on. "Cream and pine is light and bright. And the plants add a nice touch of greenery."

"Thank you. Mum and I decorated it ourselves." Didn't Mum say he was shy?

"Really? And what a lovely sofa," he says as he sits on our stuffed orange sofa. "I shall have to hire your services to come and do your interior design magic on my place, hahaha." Then Mark Collingridge tells me all about his apartment, and how he's been there for three months and still hasn't unpacked. Apart from his DVDs, because he loves movies. He pauses briefly to ask me if I've seen *Pirates of the Caribbean*, and before I can ask him which one, he goes on to tell me all about Johnny Depp, and did I know that Johnny Depp was an accomplished guitarist and he played on the soundtrack for *Chocolat*?

I'm sure there'll be no need to worry about conversation when Mark Collingridge is around. I don't even get the chance to offer him a drink. He seems nice, though—I'm surprised because I wouldn't have put him down as Mum's type.

". . . he's ever such a big fan of the Rolling Stones." Mark Collingridge is still in full flow as Mum comes into the room. "Jane, hello." Mark Collingridge jumps up and strides over to her. I think he's going to kiss her on the lips, which would be a bit icky. Well, icky for me. Then he ducks lower at the last moment and pecks her on the cheek, instead.

"Mark," Mum says as she kisses his cheek, too. Then, looking a bit embarrassed, she adds, "How are you two getting along?"

"Just brilliant," Mark Collingridge says, winking at me. "I think we're going to be great friends. Jane, you look gorgeous. As ever."

"Get away with you, you old flatterer," Mum says, and I think she's blushing, which is odd because loads of men notice Mum and she doesn't usually blush. Which makes me think of me blushing yesterday when Joe was talking to me.

Then, after a couple of minutes of chatting to me about what I am going to do tonight (worry, although I don't say that), what's in the freezer for me to eat (I know I've been ravenous lately but how can I eat at a time like this?), how the table is booked for eight and they ought to make a move, and Mum fussing with her hair and her jacket, they're off.

And just as I am thinking, what *am* I going to do with myself, Mum comes running back into the room and takes my hand. "So what do you think?" she asks, all anxious.

"I like him," I say. Because I do. Even though I think that his chatting might tire me out after five minutes. "Now, go get in that car."

I wonder if she is already in love with Mark Collingridge and if it's too late for William Brown.

Chapter 7

ACTS ABOUT ESP

1. There are too many different types of it! Including clairalience, the ability to smell ghosts (yuck!), and retrocognition, the ability to sense something (probably horrible) that happened in the past. And clairgustance, the ability to taste ghosts (also yuck)! Who knew?
2. Scientists are torn about whether ESP exists because there isn't an easy and reliable replicable laboratory experiment to prove it.
3. There are no known people with real ESP. That's a no-brainer, because if a person *did* have ESP, why would they tell anyone? They'd be a science experiment for the rest of their life!
4. A couple in England think their dog has it because whenever one of them is either (a) leaving the

house, or (b) arriving home, he runs to the porch in advance.

"Which means that cats can get ESP, too," I tell Daphne Kat, as she pumps her claws in and out of one of the cushions on the couch, but she ignores me. "Some help you are," I add, and go back to the job at hand.

My task: Find out as much as I can about ESP powers before contacting William Brown. Also, find out how to contact William Brown without him knowing who I am, so that I can assess him.

I pick up Gina's report on William Brown and read through it again.

WB FINDINGS BY GINA HEATHER DUFFY
(copyright)

About Funktech: Founded 1997 by WB and Douglas Freiman.

Description: Funktech produces computer software and technology-related products such as funky memory sticks and cell-phone cases.

About WB: Age thirty-seven, born and raised in New Jersey, USA; he attended MIT in Boston (he is smart ☺). After leaving school with a master's degree in computer science, he and Douglas Freiman formed a stockbroker company and were known in Manhattan as the Awesome Twosome because of their *uncanny ability* to sniff the sweet smell of success. ☺ (So, stockbroking being in the family—i.e., you joining Theoretical Stockbroker club—is a good indicator that he really might be your you-know-what.)

Once they made their own personal fortunes, WB and DF

quit the stockbroking world and formed Funktech with 100 percent of their own money. Since that time, the company's grown from strength to strength, and in 2002, they floated some of the shares (only 30 percent because they wanted to keep control of the company, which is smart). And now they are worth millions! (Not that you are hoping that WB is worth millions just because he might be your you-know-what ☺.)

Anyway, as far as I can see, he's single! Never been married ☺! I can't understand why he hasn't been snapped up. Unless he is either (a) still pining for your mother, (b) anti-marriage, or (c) gay. Although your existence would mean that (c) is incorrect. Well, probably. One possible fly in the ointment—I found a news report online of him attending an important finance banquet—I've listed the URL below. But be warned—there's a photo and he has a hot blonde with him.

I've also printed off last year's financial report on Funktech. It's hard to understand, but you're good at that kind of thing and I'm not.

One last snippet that you will find very interesting: WB bought a penthouse apartment in the West End of London earlier this year, and he's mainly based here! So, don't you see? It's a sign that he's your you-know-what. You both live in the same city! You were meant to find each other!

☺☺☺☺☺☺☺☺☺☺☺☺☺☺☺

I wish I had Gina's optimism.

See, William Brown is a millionaire bachelor CEO, who has penthouse apartments and gorgeous girlfriends with blond hair. So why would he want a secret daughter in his life?

I type the URL from Gina's report into my browser, and

up pops the photo of William Brown and Jessica Waterstone (a "friend" according to the newspaper piece). I spend a long time gazing at his picture on my computer screen because this one doesn't jump out and talk to me about scary stuff.

I wonder if you are my dad, William Brown. . . .

I am still staring at it when Gina calls me just after 9:00.

"So, I've been checking the financial news and guess what? Gordon Sherman passed away earlier this week, which is sad, but he was eighty-eight, which is pretty minty. Anyway, there's a special memorial service for him at Westminster Abbey tomorrow afternoon, and we should totally go."

"Um, why?" I'm a bit confused. I mean, I know who Gordon Sherman is because of my avid reading of the financial news. He founded the Independent Bank and helps—or rather helped—women in third-world countries by making them small business loans. Even having enough to purchase a mobile phone can help women empower themselves. If nobody else in your village has a mobile phone, they're going to want to either pay you or barter services with you if they need to make a call. I think Mr. Sherman was a great man, but why would I attend his memorial service?

"Because in his role as a leader in the corporate world, anybody who's anybody will be there. Your secret you-know-who? Hint, hint."

My William Brown?

"Gina, you're a genius!" I could get a look at William Brown from a safe distance, a win-win situation. Then a thought occurs to me. "How do we know that William Brown will even be there?"

"Didn't you check Funktech's homepage? There's a

personal tribute from you-know-who to Gordon Sherman. So I'm betting he'll be there. What have you got to lose?"

Gina's right. Although the possibility of seeing William Brown in the flesh is kind of nerve-racking.

"Anyway, the memorial service is at two in the afternoon, so we should plan to be there about one so we can watch all the people arrive. Why don't you come round about noon? We can have lunch before we leave. Joe's going to be here, too."

"Oh." I remember that amidst all the William Brown Talking Head worry, I haven't e-mailed Joe yet. How could I forget him?

"Yes, I thought that might interest you. Okay, it's all set. I need to go work on my slang report for Kieran. See you tomorrow.

When we hang up I realize what she said about Joe.

Does Gina know about my feelings for Joe?

More worryingly, *does Joe know*?

How does Gina know? I mean, is it because I'm somehow projecting ESP love vibes for Joe every time I think about him or see him? Or is it because in her role as my best friend she can read my secret emotions?

Whenever I'm at her house and Joe's there, too, I hardly speak to him. Except for the usual kinds of things people say to each other. And my really dorky comments when I forget about Total Anonymity due to his Presence. Like a few weeks ago when Gina and I were doing our math homework in Gina's kitchen, and Brian and Joe came to get a snack. Brian was all, "How could they declassify Pluto as a planet? It's round and it orbits the sun. That's sizeist!" and I thought Joe made a great point when he said, "Brian, mate, get over it. There are other planets equally as large as Pluto in the Kuiper belt. Should they be classified as planets, too?"

Then he turned to Gina and me and asked what we thought. Gina didn't think she was going to lose any sleep over it, and what difference did it make? But I remembered something about Pluto and wondered if I should say anything. "Well, I don't know," I said. Then, before I could stop myself, "But if you could magically change its orbit to be nearer the sun—say Earth's orbit—all of Pluto's ice would melt and it would grow a tail. Like a comet. So it wouldn't be very planetlike." All three of them stared at me in astonishment, as if I'd grown a tail. It's not exactly the kind of thing a girl would say to a boy if she liked him, is it? He'd think she was a geek!

"If I were superstitious I'd read between the lines and think that we're made for each other," I tell Daphne Kat as she pads across the sofa and looks at my computer screen. I've finally gotten my nerve up to send him my e-mail address. "I mean, his e-mail name is OccamsRazor! Gina would say it was a sign. What do you think?"

Daphne Kat just looks at me in that mysterious way of hers. She's right. I'm delusional. Joe has Melissa Stevens.

Anyway, it took me a whole hour to write my e-mail to him. Can you believe it? I was quite worried about revealing my, you know, True Feelings.

To: "Joe Summers" <OccamsRazor@sciencenet.com>
From: "Fiona Blount" <MarieCurieGirl@bluesky.com>
Subject: Theoretical Stockbroker club

Hi Joe,

Yesterday you asked me to send you my e-mail, so
here it is. Have a great weekend.

Fiona

I mean, *a whole hour* and this is the best I could come up
with?

He really will think that I am pathetic. Especially as this is
Saturday night, the hottest date night of the week, and I obviously have no date or any other kind of social plans.

I nearly fall off the sofa when Joe e-mails me back!

To: "Fiona Blount" <MarieCurieGirl@bluesky.com>
From: "Joe Summers" <OccamsRazor@sciencenet.com>
Subject: Re: Theoretical Stockbroker club

Hey Marie Curie Girl,

Marie Curie:

1. Winner of two Nobel Prizes in Science: Aymayzing.
2. That the Nobel Prizes were in two separate fields of
   science: Ultra Aymayzing.
3. Didn't patent her radium isolation process so that the
   scientific community could research it unhindered:
   Priceless!

Very cool e-mail ID. Very cool lady.

I've attached all the Theoretical Stockbroker club info for you to have a look at. If you need any help with it, you can e-mail me. Or call me.

Joe

PS. Doing anything interesting this weekend? I helped my dad with his research today (he's a physicist and into string theory). Tomorrow I'm hanging with Brian.
PPS. I've just checked—I'm still me (if you know what I mean).

Not only is Joe Summers home on a Saturday night, he also wants to know my plans for the weekend? I mean, how friendly is that? Although I already knew he was planning to hang with Brian.

His PPS makes me smile. And blush because it shows that he remembered every word of our conversation by the lockers yesterday, when I said, "Oh, it's you," and he said, "Yeah, I'm still me." It's etched in my memory! But does he mean that Marie Curie is cool, or that MarieCurieGirl (me) is cool? Or both? Oh, what shall I say back to him?

To: "Joe Summers" <OccamsRazor@sciencenet.com>
From: "Fiona Blount" <MarieCurieGirl@bluesky.com>
Subject: Re: Theoretical Stockbroker club

Hi, Still You,

<<OccamsRazor said: Didn't patent her radium isolation

process so that the scientific community could research it unhindered: Priceless!>>

Sir Tim Berners-Lee:
1. Built ENQUIRE—prototype computer communications system: Aymayzing.
2. Used similar basis to create the World Wide Web: Ultra Aymayzing.
3. Made his idea freely available to all, resulting in the Internet: Priceless!

<<I helped my dad with his research today (he's a physicist and into string theory). Tomorrow I'm hanging with Brian.>>

Quantum!

<<Doing anything interesting this weekend?>>

Oh, nothing interesting. Just trying to read my cat's mind. And tomorrow Gina and I have plans.

Fiona
_____

"How lame does that sound?" I ask Daphne Kat. She brushes her head against my arm. "Do you think it sounds like I'm flirting?" Joe will think I'm an idiot. Plus, he will think I've lost it completely with that comment about trying to read Daphne's mind.

Oh. My. God. He's e-mailed me back already!

To: "Fiona Blount" <MarieCurieGirl@bluesky.com>
From: "Joe Summers" <OccamsRazor@sciencenet.com>
Subject: Re: Theoretical Stockbroker club

Re: Tim Berners-Lee. Totally agree—another personal
icon. Good luck with your cat—I have the same
problem with our cat, Pasteur (named for Louis
Pasteur, of course—Mum's choice). Gotta go—TTYL!

Still Me

That blows my Saturday-night theory out of the water. I
wonder if he's off to meet Melissa Stevens. . . .

But he did say TTYL, so does that mean I should e-mail him
back and he'll talk back to me later? Or is he just being nice?
Logically I must conclude that he is just being nice. I mean,
anybody who has a cat for a pet must be nice by definition!

I am still worrying about this (and everything else) when
Mum floats in on a cloud of post-date Mark Collingridge
euphoria. I wonder if I look like that when I am either thinking about or speaking with Joe?

"Hey, Fabulous Fiona. Did you have a good evening?
What did you do?" Mum is positively girly as she flops down
beside me on the big orange sofa.

"I had a great time hanging with Daphne Kat," I tell her.
"We chased a few pens, had tuna for supper, then tried to read
each other's minds. The usual stuff." That makes her laugh.

Then, because I need to find out the extent of her feelings
for Mark Collingridge, I say, "Did you have a nice time with
Mark Collingridge?"

"It was lovely. We went to Lannigan's in Hampstead," she says, relaxing her head back against the sofa and closing her eyes.

Lannigan's? That's a really posh restaurant. I know this because I have a clipping about it in my "possible investments" folder. You have to make reservations weeks in advance for a Saturday-night table, therefore (a) Mark must really like my mum, and (b) they have been dating for longer than I thought! So I encourage her to tell me more about him, because although chatty, he didn't tell me anything about himself.

"Mark's so funny. And interesting." Then she tells me that he's a guitarist—a session musician—and he's played with practically the entire music industry. Even on *Bliss Babes Forever*, which was their second album. That's how Mum met him ten years ago. It was the album that shot the Bliss Babes onto the charts for the first time, and the guitar riff on "Destructor Toy," their first hit single, was all down to Mark.

"Seriously, Fiona." Mum sits up and turns to face me. "What do you think of him? Did you mean what you said, earlier? Because he's shy with new people, and he worried he'd made a fool of himself."

"He didn't seem shy to me. He's a bit of a talker." I smile as I say this because she looks anxious. About me liking him.

"He does talk a lot when he's nervous." She laughs. "Especially about movies—he's quite the film buff."

"Well, he seems nice." Which is the truth, but I really need to find out how much she likes him.

"Mum, can I ask you something?" If I'm going to try and find out if William Brown is my dad or not, then I should at least give her some warning because if she's in love with

Mark Collingridge and I drag William Brown into our lives, I might create a Love Triangle! "Um, do you ever think about William Brown?"

I kind of wish I hadn't asked because Mum gets all flustered. "Fiona, what's brought this on? Is it because I'm dating Mark? Mark's a great guy, but we're just dating right now. We're not setting wedding dates or anything."

"No, it's not that. I just . . . wondered." *Lame excuse, Fiona,* I think. But I can hardly tell her the truth. "You know, if William Brown turned up on the doorstep, *pouf,* out of the blue, do you think you'd still love him? Do you think he ever wonders if he has a secret daughter or son?"

Mum looks at me for a long time and then she says, "I used to think about him a lot, but it's been fifteen years. We barely knew each other, we were little more than kids, and people change. They move on with their lives, they have to. Otherwise they . . . miss opportunities. I don't think it would have occurred to him that I was pregnant, either, because we used protection."

They did? So William Brown really wouldn't have an inkling that he might have a theoretical offspring.

"Well, it's nice for a girl to know that her mother practices safe sex," I say to lighten up the situation. "But that might be too much information." And we both laugh.

"I think of you as my ten-to-twenty-percent miracle," she says. "Is this worrying you? That you don't know your dad? I've told you before that if you want we could try and track him down and I mean it. I could hire a private investigator—"

"All we have to go on is an old photo, a common name, and a few facts." I shake my head. "So it would be a huge wild goose chase." The last thing I want is for Mum to spend lots of money on a private investigator when I might have found him for free. Mum still looks worried so I squeeze her hand and smile reassuringly, which I think makes her feel better. "Anyway, we're the Blount girls against the world."

But I have another worrying thought. William Brown has ESP and knows other people with ESP. Couldn't he have used it to find Mum? Didn't he want to find her?

Can we say *utter disappointment*?

"There's still time for you-know-who to show." Gina is far more optimistic than I. No girl ever had a better friend!

We've been standing here on Broad Sanctuary, just off Parliament Square, in the driving rain for nearly an hour, and there has been no sign of William Brown. We've seen quite a lot of other people, including famous ones like Prince Harry (representing the royal family), but not William Brown. Not that I really expected to be able to pick him out, because Gordon Sherman was such an important man and there's a large crowd attending the service. Most of the area surrounding the entrance to the Abbey has been cordoned off by the police, too, so it's hard to get a good view. I think it's hopeless!

I haven't said this to Gina on account of not wanting to hurt her feelings about her plan. It would be nice for a girl to see her possible father, though, once in her life. William Brown looks so lovely from his photo and talking head. I bet he's really lovely in real life, too, because anybody who was friends with a philanthropist like Gordon Sherman is bound to be, isn't he? Or is that just wishful thinking on my part?

Lovely and wishful thinking reminds me of what happened at Gina's house earlier, when Joe was there. I was embarrassed at first because I worried that I was emitting love vibes or something. And I had to be careful to keep my expression inscrutable—just in case, you know, it showed my love for him. I had practiced in front of the mirror at home for maximum inscrutability.

As Gina and I were eating her mum's homemade broccoli soup, Brian and Joe came into the kitchen. That made me lose my appetite straightaway. What was I going to say to Joe? But I needn't have worried—Brian was going on about loop quantum gravity making more sense to him than the other alternatives, and where was the proof?

"Yes, but string theory seems to be able to unify the known natural forces. How do you explain that?" Joe told him as he sat down next to me. I tried not to shiver. Gina gave me one of her knowing glances, and I felt even more flustered.

Joe and Brian went on about D-branes and NS-branes, and how great it would be if only a consistent theory of quantum gravity could be discovered. Gina shook her head in disgust. "It's all mysterious to me," she said. And before I could stop myself, I told her that the Large Hadron Collider in Switzerland might provide some evidence once it's finished. Okay, I've been reading up on quantum mechanics (because of Joe). That was a conversation killer, I can tell you, because all three of them looked at me as if I'd arrived from Mars.

"How do you know these things? You're a girl, you're supposed to spend your time yearning for the boy of your dreams. And fashion and normal stuff." Brian only said that to get a rise out of his sister. But I just blushed. Honestly, how nerdy did I sound?

"Fiona isn't a normal girl," Gina said, which I *think* is a compliment. The ESP part is definitely not normal.

"Not being normal is a good thing, Marie Curie Girl," Joe told me, and I'm sure my face went red. I *love* that he called me Marie Curie Girl.

Before I could find my tongue, Gina said it was time to leave for the service.

And it was due to start in about two minutes.

"Never mind," Gina says, patting my arm. "So, we didn't see you-know-who enter, but maybe we'll see him when he leaves."

"You know what I think?" I tell Gina as another blast of wind hits us, nearly blowing us and the whole crowd of onlookers off our feet. "I think we should wait until Big Ben chimes the hour, then go home. It was a great plan, though, thank you for thinking of it."

The look of relief on Gina's face is plain. "We'll come up with a better William Brown plan, too, I just know we will."

As Big Ben chimes its first chord, I get a prickle at the back of my neck. Then, when Big Ben chimes again, a large black limousine pulls up on the corner near the entrance to Westminster Abbey. The prickle turns into a tingle. Just like the first time I saw William Brown Talking Head! When the chauffeur opens the door, the huge, enormous, tingle becomes a loud, deafening roar, and someone climbs out.

It's William Brown!!

"Oh. My. God. *It's him!*" Gina's voice is a squeak.

My stomach is fluttering with nerves. I can hardly breathe. I can't take my eyes off him. As he helps his female companion—who very much resembles the blonde in the online photo—out of the limousine I can only see the side of his face. I wish he'd stand up and face me, so that I can get a proper look at him.

They turn to walk to the entrance, and all I can see is his back.

I have to try to make him turn around! I may never get the chance again. So I'm wishing with all my heart, with everything I have, that he will TURN AROUND and LOOK AT ME. The blood is pounding in my brain, my stomach is heaving, and I'm throwing every single bit of my longing at him. The pressure in my head builds till I can barely stand. And then the pressure vanishes, and I stagger.

But it doesn't work. My ESP has obviously deserted me.

Sadly I still have a throbbing head and I feel sick. Really sick. And all for nothing.

Then William Brown stops in his tracks as he reaches the entrance. He turns around and scans the street, as if he's searching for someone.

The blond woman speaks to him, and he shakes his head. Then they both walk into Westminster Abbey.

"If I were superstitious I'd say that was a bit spooky," Gina comments. "Like he was looking for somebody." Then, when she looks at me, she says, "You look terrible."

I pull away from her and run around the corner to a quieter street (not that any streets around here are particularly quiet).

And puke.

What does it all mean?

Chapter 8

"**A**re you going to mention you-know-who to your mum?" Gina whispers to me during lunchbreak at school. She was concerned on Sunday when I threw up and said that since I hadn't finished my broccoli soup at lunch, my energy level was low, and the shock of seeing my probable father was the last straw.

Honestly my life would be so much simpler if William Brown 57 from my fact file were my father. Although sharing WB 57's life as a hermit in a small, frugal cottage on a small Scottish island wouldn't be very comfortable, it would be more straightforward.

"I don't know." I sigh morosely. It's been three days since our William Brown sighting, and I'm more confused than ever! Did he sense me there in the crowd, or was that just my imagination? What is my next step? "She's totally gearing up for the concert, figuring out things like is Madonna definitely on board? It just seems unfair to give Mum more to worry about at the moment."

Peaceflower, who seems a bit distracted and so far has been quietly eating her lunch of alfalfa salad, chooses this moment to catch up with the conversation. I'd almost forgotten she was there. "Madonna?" she squeaks loudly. Before Gina and I can tell her to keep her voice down, on account of not wanting to attract attention, she adds, "Do you mean *the* Madonna? Your mother knows Madonna? The pop star? That's so cool!" And she's off, chattering about why she thinks Madonna is a great businesswoman as well as a talented performer, and what an inspiration she is to womankind, which is true, but unfortunately everyone at the nearby tables is looking at us. Oh, no, here we go again!

Melissa Stevens who, of course, has overheard every word, is all, "You have got to be kidding me," as she rolls her eyes at Suzy Langton. But Chaz Peterson thinks it's supremely minty, and can I get Madonna's autograph for him? Suzy slaps him on the arm and glares at me.

"Um, it's a different Madonna," I say, which sounds a bit lame. It's all I can think of. But this bit of notoriety has given me a taste of how different life at school will be when Mum announces her charity concert on TV and people figure out that Mum is, you know, *my mum*, which depresses me even more and I slump down in my seat.

If only I could rewind the clock!

Melissa and Suzy are talking about what losers we are, and how could a mouse girl who hangs with a giantess (Gina, who is not *that* tall) and a hippie-dippy girl (Peaceflower) possibly have any connection to Madonna? Suzy tosses her black curls and says that Madonna is *so* nineties, although Chaz says he thinks she's a genius at reinventing herself. Which starts a whole conversation about other stars reinventing themselves. At least it means that Melissa isn't concentrating on us.

"It wasn't a different Madonna, was it?" Peaceflower asks me finally.

"No," I tell her. "You got the right one. It's just that people like me have to keep a low profile. You know, to avoid attention."

"I'm sorry. I got the wrong end of the stick. I'm always getting the wrong end of the stick. I wish my parents had never moved here," she adds, cuddling her orange, flowered backpack for comfort.

I tell her that I know only too well how it feels to be moved to a different school, a different culture, and that it will be okay.

Then Peaceflower tells us that Carl has broken up with her. He just couldn't take the stress of a long-distance relationship, even though it's only been a week. Plus, he's met someone, and Celestial is the real woman of his dreams. Peaceflower was just a youthful crush. "I can be so daft," she says.

Even though Gina and I make it clear that she is not stupid, that she just needs time to adjust, and that what she is feeling is homesickness for all of her old friends, Peaceflower's still miserable. We assure her that Carl is a complete idiot and it's his loss, not hers, and there are plenty more fish in the sea. But she's still miserable.

"And now we're your new friends," I tell her. "Aren't we, Gina?"

"Most emphatically." Gina nods. "But if you want to survive around here you need to learn more about Total Anonymity."

"Yes," I say. "Like, it's important to keep your voice down in crowded places like the lunchroom."

I've been thinking about Total Anonymity and ESP a lot over the past few days, too, and have come to some tentative conclusions. I believe I've been using my ESP to help maintain Total Anonymity for years. All the times I've worried about being noticed when people like Melissa are around has been accompanied by three things: that faint tingle at the back of my head, the fear in my stomach, and the thought in my brain about not wanting to be noticed. I've been broadcasting ESP thoughts, I think. I've just got so used to it being there, it's a kind of superpowers-meets-real-world fusion.

It makes perfect sense.

But now that Peaceflower, who doesn't really understand about real-world Total Anonymity, is with us, I need to find some way of expanding my personal Total Anonymity thoughts to a higher level. So that she doesn't attract attention.

"Oh, I'm just so excited to have two proper friends!" Peaceflower squeaks, clasping her hands together, which prompts laughs from the adjacent tables. It's like complete rejection and dejection to elation in five seconds. "Oh, sorry," she whispers. "I've already forgotten that I should speak more quietly."

That's exactly what I mean.

"You'll learn," I say, hoping that I'm right. "We'll teach you."

By Wednesday afternoon I have a low-level headache due to stress from trying to work on my theory of fusion Total Anonymity. I definitely have the low-level tingle in my head, and the fear in my stomach, and the thought in my brain all working together so that when Peaceflower put her hand up in math earlier, nobody (Melissa) noticed! Even so, I'm not in the mood for Theoretical Stockbroker club.

Just before last period Gina, Peaceflower, and I find Gaynor Cole crying in the loo. When I say crying, I mean she's sobbing in the stall, and we can't leave her there, can we?

"I can't tell you." Gaynor is sobbing over and over again, and we're trying to calm her down from the other side of the stall door. "They'll do something—I can't tell you that, either." She won't open the stall door until we swear on everything sacred that Melissa and Suzy aren't anywhere in the immediate vicinity. I mean, we have a pretty good idea who "they" are.

"Here." Peaceflower rummages in her backpack, pulls out a ruby crystal, and holds it under the stall door. "This will really help you, Gaynor. It's a crystal to help with fear and sadness. Concentrate on the crystal," Peaceflower implores her. Gina rolls her eyes at me over Peaceflower's head, but I think having a crystal to focus on is rather a good idea—and Peaceflower means well. "Hold it and concentrate. The vibrations of the crystal will focus your fear and diffuse it. It really helped me cope with my loss of Carl."

"I don't think there's a crystal big enough on earth to save me." Gaynor hiccups and takes the crystal. A few seconds later she opens the door. Poor thing, her face is all blotchy from crying, which doesn't help her acne. But at least she's not sobbing anymore.

We take Gaynor to Mrs. Hunter, because it's clear that she needs to go home. She can't stop shaking! We tell Mrs. Hunter that Gaynor is sick (which is not a lie but is not the whole truth—Gaynor is sick with worry and fear). Of course, Mrs. Hunter isn't the most sympathetic soul in the world because she's probably missing a vital soap on TV, or something. As she's telling Gaynor that she's making a fuss about nothing, all us girls are the same, and it's just that time of month (her standard explanation), I remind her that even people who get arrested are allowed one phone call. She didn't like that much, but she tutted and handed Gaynor the telephone so that she could call her mum to come and get her.

As I head to my first meeting of Theoretical Stockbroker club, I am still worrying about what they could have done to poor Gaynor to get her into such a state. It must be serious if she can't talk about it. And I'm nervous about Theoretical Stockbroker club, because what if it's a disaster? At least Melissa won't be able to say anything awful because Joe will be there, but I'm definitely aware of my fusion Anonymity right now.

"Hey, Marie Curie Girl," Joe says from behind me, as I approach the door to the small study next to Principal Darnell's room, where the club meets. I forget about everything except how happy I am to see him. Immediately my pulse begins to race because he's right next to me. "Glad you could make it." Oh, but his smile is so cute!

I revert to type, of course. "Um, hi. Me, too." I can barely stop myself from shivering! I wish I was a conversationalist, or even just a chatterer like Peaceflower, instead of a dimwit!

Then Joe surprises me some more. "So, I noticed that you didn't get very far yesterday with your mentee." He did? I try to attain an inscrutable expression as I look up into his face. I mean, it's rude to talk to someone and not look at them, isn't it? Oh, even his hair, tufted at the front, is cute. It doesn't do my pulse any good whatsoever.

"Um, no, it didn't work out very well."

"I have an idea of how I could help you." He does? Why would he even want to bother?

"I don't think anything will help with Bev. People generally don't learn if they're under duress," I tell him, shaking my head.

"Under duress?" Joe looks surprised. "I'm sure she wants to improve her grades. I overheard her discussing it with Mr. Fenton. She really needs to pass math to move to the next grade after the summer."

"Well, maybe it's because she just can't stand me." I'm certainly not one of the Clique One girls.

"I don't think it's personal, Marie Curie Girl," Joe tells me, and he's smiling at me in a way that makes me want to shiver some more. Although I do think it is personal with Bev. "It could be that you're in the same grade, therefore part of her immediate peer group. Or she could be intimidated by your vast intellect," he adds. I'm totally shocked by how much attention he's paid to the situation, but what he says makes sense. Maybe she does want to improve her grades. And then I take in what Joe just said about my intellect.

"How can she be intimidated by my intellect? I always get Bs."

"Yes, I know." He does? "Don't panic." He laughs at my surprise. "I'm not a stalker. I heard Mrs. Duffy going on to Gina about getting Bs and Gina told her that if her best friend and major brain girl Fiona could only score Bs, then Gina scoring Bs was a major achievement. Why do you do that, by the way? You could obviously score As."

"It's a long story," I tell him, shaking my head. This boy is too observant for my peace of mind! What if he can tell that I like him?

"Anyway, this idea," he begins, just as Melissa Stevens comes running over. "Do you know Fibonacci's numbers?"

"Um, yes." I'm confused now. What on earth can something we studied in math have to do with getting Bev to let me tutor her?

"Hi, Joe, I was waiting for you by the lockers but I figured I'd missed you," Melissa says, all breathless and blond. And then she's all over him with her plans for the weekend, and how they should hang at Chaz Peterson's place because his parents' house extension is finished and Chaz has the attic to himself. She hooks Joe's arm and tugs him away, but not before she's noticed me. She flashes me a look as if to say, "Hands off," so I take a deep breath to calm myself and follow them into the room.

I guess his plan about Bev wasn't so important after all, I think, as I absorb the room dynamics. Suzy and Chaz are making out in the back of the room, which grosses me out. I mean, I can see their tongues! Nicholas Bergin and Harry Emond, computer nerds, are playing some kind of war game on Nicholas's laptop. Plus there are three guys I know by sight—Buzz Jackson (because of his buzz haircut), the lead singer of the resident school rock band; Nigel "the Whiz" Corrie, a whiz at science and cool into the bargain—much like Joe—and Luiz Harani, who hangs with Gina's Kieran.

"We have a new member," Joe says as everyone comes and sits down in a circle, then he introduces me. Melissa sits on one side of Joe, indicating to Suzy that she should sit on his other side. Then she glares at me. I mean, why bother? It's not like I'm a threat to Joe's affection for her. As the rest of the seats fill up, I have the choice of either sitting next to Melissa or next to Buzz, leaving a gap of one seat between Melissa and me. Buzz is the safer choice.

"Two new members, I mean," Joe adds as another figure appears in the doorway. "Come on in, Mike."

Fat Mike, of course, takes the only seat left between Melissa and me. Melissa is all, "Hi, Mike, we're so glad you could join us," and smiles her fake smile. I try to fade into the background as Joe opens the meeting. Joe does a lot of the talking and this is a perfect opportunity to watch My Love with a good excuse (but I'm careful to keep my expression inscrutable). Then everyone does a brief presentation on his or her proposal (not Mike and me this week, because we're getting the feel of things). After that everyone votes. Unfortunately for Melissa, everyone votes no for her soft-toy company. Except for Suzy and Chaz, of course. I mean, the toys are cute, but didn't she read the company's last quarter report?

"It could have been worse, I suppose," Fat Mike tells me in his gloom-and-doom voice when the meeting ends and Melissa's all over Joe again. I hope Mike's not in love with Melissa because he's watching them a bit sadly. "At least nobody called me Fat Mike." And you know what? It just strikes me as sad and wrong that a person can derive comfort from someone *not* being mean to them. And that I should stop referring to him as Fat Mike. It also strikes me that I don't know what Joe meant when he asked me about Fibonacci's numbers.

Exactly the same thing happens in Mentoring Minds on Thursday with Bev. She's reading a magazine, and I'm concentrating on Ms. Maldine, who still has a mustache. I also have my hand on Peaceflower's crystal in my pocket. If I focus my thoughts on the crystal as a central point, maybe I can get this to work . . . if only I could get a tingle.

I concentrate even harder on how the tingle feels. But it won't work. I think of how much I can't stand Melissa, who I saw talking to Gaynor Cole in English earlier. Ms. Woods was too busy trying to engage a class of thirty kids in *Flowers for Algernon*, the book we're supposed to read before next week. Melissa was smiling smugly, but Gaynor was visibly shaking as she handed over a manila folder to her.

It made me feel so angry and powerless, but by the time I'd begun to feel angry enough to get stronger prickles, Melissa was back in her seat.

Remembering the incident now works, though. The tingles begin, and I squeeze the crystal in my pocket even harder as I look at Ms. Maldine. I get the familiar black dots in my vision, so I take a deep breath and try to calm myself a little. I don't want to end up fainting or vomiting in the middle of the library.

Carefully, I think, USE A WAX STRIP ON YOUR MUSTACHE, USE A WAX STRIP ON YOUR MUSTACHE, but not too hard. All of a sudden I get this quiet buzzing in my ears, more like a whisper, and I focus even harder on the crystal as I imagine Ms. Maldine with a wax strip above her mouth. Just as I am about to give up, Ms. Maldine glances up from her book and touches her mustache!

Then someone drags a chair over and sits opposite me, and I forget all about crystals and Ms. Maldine's mustache. It's Joe!

"Question for you, Marie Curie Girl." He leans his arms on my desk and rests his chin on his hands, so that he is looking into my face. I stifle a little gasp as my pulse begins to race. I glance around the room, but everybody is busy doing their thing.

"Fire away, Still Me," I surprise myself by saying, and then surprise myself even more when I lean my arms on my desk as well and rest my chin on them.

"Kieran and I are having a debate about whether boys are smarter than girls at math and science, because of their bigger brains—"

"Oh, I'd have to disagree, because you know size isn't everything." *Oh. My. God.* Did I just say that? I can feel my ears getting hot. But Joe is laughing.

"Exactly what I said. So back to the question. If I were to give you this string of numbers—0, 1, 1, 2, 3, 5, 8—would it mean anything to you?"

"Leonardo of Pisa," I say, grinning. "Otherwise known as Fibonacci, famous for the Fibonacci numbers. That string you quoted is the opening sequence."

"Bingo!" Joe says, sitting up. And just as I am getting this really fuzzy warm feeling in the pit of my stomach, he turns to Bev. Who I had momentarily forgotten about and who is watching us.

"You're really lucky to have Fiona mentor you, Bev," he tells her. Then he slides his chair back to his desk.

I turn back to my textbook more than a little deflated because I know why Joe did what he did, and it wasn't because he was flirting with me or anything. Bev is looking at me very strangely. Plus, do I actually want this girl to think I'm smart? Won't she tell Melissa?

"Okay." Bev turns to me, and I try not to focus on how much I don't like her. "You, like, really get this quadratic equation stuff?"

"Yes. Um, do you want me to show you?"

"You think that even *I* could learn this?" Bev asks me, and I can tell from the eagerness in her tone that she genuinely wants to improve her math grade.

"Of course. It's just a matter of breaking it down into sizable chunks and understanding what the math terms actually mean."

"That would be so cool—if I could raise my grade by only one point my parents would be thrilled," she says, smiling at me.

Somehow I hadn't thought of Bev as the kind of person who wanted to please her parents. It kind of makes her more . . . human. Before I can stop myself I'm smiling back at her.

And then we remember our positions in the cliquing order and she scowls at me.

"Anyway, I've finished my magazine," she says, shrugging. "I guess it beats boredom."

Chapter 9

Peaceflower arrived at school with her acoustic guitar this morning in a case covered in flower stickers (not a surprise), all enthusiastic about earning SACS points in the school band. She just wasn't hearing Gina and me when we stressed the importance of Total Anonymity, and how auditioning for one of the school bands was not a way to achieve it.

Peaceflower was all, "Oh, I have to find some way of earning SACS points, and I'm not clever so I can't mentor. I'm rubbish at understanding the stock market. And acting, which rules out drama club. So what's left? And Buzz, the lead singer of the rock group, is cute!"

I felt a bit mean for raining on her parade. I am also thinking that she got over Carl very quickly, because it's only been a few days.

"Nobody ever remembers the guitarist in a band," Gina said brightly, and I immediately thought of The Edge, and

Keith Richards, and Jimmy Page, but then I thought that I only knew about them because of music (even old music) playing a big part in Mum's life, therefore a big part in mine, too. "And it would keep us out of the lunchroom because as your friends we will be there to support you," Gina added, giving me a meaningful stare.

She has a point. It would be an effective way of staying out of the lunchroom when Mean Melissa and Gang are there.

When we arrive in the crowded gym, we realize how wrong we were on both counts. It is packed with hopeful musicians and singers, all hoping to join the brass band, or the rock band, or the folk group. Who knew so many students are interested in music?

But the biggest shock is that Melissa is currently auditioning for the rock band, singing a Britney Spears song, "Oops! . . . I Did It Again," with Suzy and Bev as her backing singers, of course. No offense to Britney but it's kind of so 2000. Plus, Melissa's voice is a little flat. I get instant prickles.

Gina and I look at each other. Gina closes her eyes briefly and swallows. I know how she feels. I clutch the crystal in my pocket as I feel the fear in my stomach. *Total Anonymity*, I think. *Don't let Melissa notice us.*

It's too late to leave because Mr. Barani, the music teacher, comes over to talk to Peaceflower as soon as he sees she's carrying her guitar. When Melissa finishes doing it again, everyone cheers and claps, and she's bowing.

As she, Suzy, and Bev strut off the stage and head for Mr. Barani, who's telling Peaceflower to go and join people auditioning for the folk group in the far side of the gym, I'm clutching the crystal so tight that it's almost cutting into my hand.

"So, what did you think, Mr. Barani?" Melissa's all smiling and expectant. "Wasn't that like the best Britney impression you've ever seen? So, we're in the band?" So far, she's not even registering us. I just wish Peaceflower would do what Mr. Barani said and move to the far corner of the gym, but she doesn't.

"I'll let you know." Mr. Barani smiles at them, then turns to Peaceflower.

"Um, I actually came to join the rock band, not the folk group," Peaceflower says, and my heart sinks into my feet as Melissa notices her. Melissa's face is all disbelief as she checks out Peaceflower's flower-covered guitar case, and then she laughs. Then Melissa notices us. "Don't tell me, you two are auditioning for rock band, too? That would just make my day." And then she and Suzy laugh. Bev doesn't, though. This is exactly what I mean about Total Anonymity not working once the person has deliberately attracted attention to themselves!

Mr. Barani doesn't seem too sure about Peaceflower's request, but he sends her over to the position Melissa has just vacated.

I can tell that Buzz and the guys are skeptical, too, because Buzz looks Peaceflower up and down with disbelief. Despite the lesson in Total Anonymity on school uniform, and the list of stores that stock the real uniform instead of her homemade uniform, she's still wearing the too-long skirt and the too-big jacket.

Buzz glances over his shoulder at the five other guys. They all look pretty shocked. Like, you've got to be kidding me. "We don't do folk music or any acoustic guitar stuff," Buzz tells her, eyeing her flowered guitar case. "We're the rock element. We do stuff like The Killers, Green Day, and The White Stripes. And our own stuff. Strictly no Joni Mitchell."

Peaceflower isn't fazed at all. "That's okay, I can do other things. But I'll have to borrow that electric guitar." Buzz looks over his shoulder at the band again, and they're kind of smirking and shrugging in a way that suggests (a) Peaceflower is mad, and (b) let the girl do her stuff, anyway.

"This, I have *got* to see. Come on, girls, let's take a seat," Melissa says, and walks to the bleachers on one side of the gym.

I glance at Gina. "This isn't going to be pretty."

"I know." Gina shakes her head. What else can we do? We take seats on the bleachers, too, as far away from Melissa and Gang as we can manage. Then Peaceflower begins.

Let's just say that nobody is smirking two minutes later.

She starts with "Somebody Told Me" by The Killers, and after about twenty seconds Buzz adds the vocals. We all listen with our mouths wide-open. By the time she's a minute into the song, the entire rock band has joined in with her. Everyone else in the gym has stopped what they are doing and is listening in amazement!

"Who knew she'd be so good?" I mean, you wouldn't guess by looking at her. First tennis and now this. Peaceflower is full of surprises.

"I know," Gina says as Peaceflower sways and bangs her head along to the music.

When the song ends, and everyone's crying "Encore," Buzz asks Peaceflower if she knows "Crazy" by Gnarls Barkley, which is more pop than strictly rock. It's when Peaceflower nods and asks him if he wants her to pick out the violin part, too, because the guitar part isn't that demanding, that I feel sick and scared.

Mr. Barani is looking at Peaceflower as if he can't believe his good luck. The band members seem pretty impressed, too. As Buzz is crooning away that his girl is driving him crazy, the prickles get stronger. I risk a glance at Melissa. Her arms are folded across her chest, and her lips are pursed. She's definitely not happy.

"Uh-oh," Gina says as Melissa stands up and puts a hand on her hip. "Trouble alert."

The tingles at the back of my neck intensify as my stomach spasms, and I'm thinking, *Oh no, here we go again.* Melissa will have a total field day with this! I'm breaking out in a cold sweat. Melissa might do something really bad to Peaceflower for being, you know, better than Melissa at another thing. What that bad something might be, I don't know, but it's just not fair!

I'm really thinking hard, FORGET PEACEFLOWER, LEAVE THE ROOM RIGHT NOW. I can't control myself! I grab the crystal in my pocket and suddenly my head is filled with pressure, and I get the familiar black spots in my vision. I feel like I'm going to fly apart any second!

Then it happens. As the pressure leaves my brain, Melissa's eyes go blank—zombielike—*and she really does leave the room!* Suzy and Bev are watching her as if they can't believe their eyes, but they get up and follow her, too.

"Tell your friend she should stay away from Melissa," Bev warns me as she passes me, and I'm shocked she feels even a pang of concern for Peaceflower. "Things could get ugly."

I slump in my seat, exhausted and sick, my head pounding.

"What just happened there?" Gina asks me.

"Um, maybe Melissa was jealous and couldn't cope with Peaceflower's talent?" I say.

"You know, Fiona, you don't look so good."

I don't feel so good, either. I really do need to find out what is going on in my head! If only I could think straight.

"And you know what else?" Gina adds, peering at me closely. "Don't you think it's a bit odd that weird things have been happening recently? Like the other day at the memorial service when William Brown seemed to be looking for someone in the crowd? Like just now with Melissa? I so thought she was going to make trouble, but she stopped. Then simultaneously you get sick and headachey."

"It's just a coincidence," I tell her, but I don't think she believes me because of the quizzical expression on her face.

"You'll tell me when you're ready," she says, patting my hand. "I think you need two Tylenol."

Now, on top of everything else, I have to worry about Gina's natural perceptiveness!

Chapter 10

On Saturday, after having a strange dream I cannot even bear to think about, for reasons both good and bad, I have *three* epiphanies about contacting William Brown. It must be my anxiety generating adrenaline to help the thinking process along!

The first one happens when Mum asks about my plans for the day over our bowls of bran and banana. I think, *More worrying about William Brown and testing out my ESP,* which I can't seem to command at will, by the way, because I can't focus unless I'm really upset. Like yesterday. After the incident in the gym, Melissa was kind of strange for the rest of the afternoon. In physical ed and the showers, she didn't even seem to know that Peaceflower, Gina, or I were even there! Have I altered her brain for life? Have I zombiefied her? I don't like her, but I don't want to give her permanent brain damage or something!

But I can't say that to Mum, can I? So when I say not much, she asks me if I want to help Sharon sort through all the promotional stuff in the studio storeroom. Mum gets so much stuff! You know, from grateful artists whose CDs she's produced and companies who want her to use their products. Anyway, they send cool stuff like fancy T-shirts or tickets to West End shows, or designer tote bags. Mum gives the stuff to her staff, but there's always loads left over. Which reminds me about certain leftover items, and how they might help me in my William Brown quest.

"Yeah, yeah." Sharon's talking to one of the concert organizers on the phone in the adjoining office, while I finish up tidying the stockroom. "Yer can definitely add Richard Branson to the sponsorship list. He's up for four tickets."

It hasn't taken very long, but I've found what I'm looking for. A guy from Virgin Records sent Mum a batch of promotional mobile phones with prepaid minutes on them. They're hot pink and covered in rhinestones. Not exactly my style.

"Yeah. Owkay. Johnny Depp's people sed he'd be interested, too. Lemme give yer the number for his people. He can't make the concert, but he's asked us to donate his tickets to charity to raise a bit more cash.

"You've done a fab job," Sharon says to me, sticking her head around the door. Then she spots the mobile in my hand. "Help yerself to anything you want, sweetheart—you'd be doin' me a favor," she says, pointing to the phone. "I can get you a different mobile phone wiv a real plan if you'd like."

"Thanks, Sharon, but these are perfect," I tell her, because a phone plan would totally ruin my first epiphany. My secret plan to ring William Brown on the talking head number. "You know how I love hot pink. And rhinestones!" She gives me a bit of a look, and then, because I had my second epiphany when Sharon was on the phone just now, I take a deep breath and tell her something else. "Um, I know of a company that might be interested in sponsoring the concert." What if I'm doing the wrong thing? I show Sharon the Funktech website, especially the part in the mission statement about being committed to helping young people in industry and the arts. Sharon says that she thinks Funktech sounds good, and before I can blink she's on the phone to the concert organizers again.

So, if William Brown does decide to sponsor the concert, and if he, you know, attends it and sees Mum, he can decide what to do next. It would prove whether he truly wanted to find her. Or not. All without Mum needing to know. All without William Brown needing to know that I have ESP, too. Or that he even has a secret daughter.

Next, I head to the Internet café on Kensington High Street, and I listen to William Brown Talking Head. It's pretty weird, me being the only one in the café able to see and hear him, and as I listen, I glance around at the other customers. Nobody notices anything! Then, when William Brown recites the telephone number I should call, I write it down. Using a public computer means that he can't trace me back to my computer.

Then I walk to Kensington Gardens, and find a peaceful spot near Kensington Palace—if I ring from a public place, it won't matter if William Brown's organization can track the phone via satellite, because it won't lead them to my house, but will lead instead to members of the royal family who live in the palace.

This is it. I'm going to call William Brown.

My fingers are trembling so badly that I can barely press in the numbers. As I listen to the ringing tone, I can hardly breathe. And when someone picks up, my heart thuds in my chest.

"Hello, friend, this is Cynthia," a pleasant-sounding woman tells me. "I'm here to help you. What's your name?"

"Um, Anne," I lie. "Can I, um, speak to William Brown?"

"Anne, Will isn't around right now, but I know why you're calling. You've seen Will's special message. You've developed ESP skills, and you're confused and worried."

"Um, yes." Of course William Brown doesn't answer the calls. How could I delude myself? He's a millionaire CEO playboy who has a lot of ESP people working for him.

"Firstly, as Will told you in his message, you're not alone anymore. You're with friends who are just like you. Why don't we meet, you and I, and I can tell you all about our organization in person."

"Actually I'm fine with the phone for now. I mean, you're a stranger."

"That's okay, Anne," Cynthia reassures me. "I can understand why you're wary."

Then Cynthia tells me that there are about one hundred people known to have ESP, and that's only the ones that have come forward. The organization is called Esper, and the people refer to themselves as espees. I'm an espee! Then she asks me what more I'd like to know.

"So, um." Where do I begin? "I seem to be able to, you know, make people do things. Not really bad things, just things like making them forget about a person if they're trying to pick on them." Then it all comes pouring out of me. I tell her about the tingles, and the pressure, and the spots in my vision, and the sickness and hunger I get afterward. About not being able to do this mental stuff when I like.

"That's all perfectly normal for an espee newbie," Cynthia assures me. It is? "You're overextending." I am? "What happens is that your brain is using a large part of your body's energy. It's draining a little bit from all over the place, or sometimes a lot from all over the place, which is why you feel so awful afterward. You're physically and mentally exhausted. Usually a good rest and a calorific meal will really help. But I have to tell you, Anne, that this overexertion is not good for you. You're draining too much energy from your body at one time, and not focusing effectively with your brain. You can actually achieve quite a lot with a small amount of energy once you learn how to do that."

"But can I, you know, permanently damage someone's brain? Turn them into a zombie, or something? By accident?"

"Well," Cynthia says after a pause, which is not reassuring. "I suppose that permanently altering someone's brain *might* be a possibility. We're not actually sure. Which is why it's a good idea to try not to use your skills until you've had the chance to practice them more and learn to focus them. It was a shock to me, too, the first time my ESP kicked in. I was forty, that was five years after the drug trial. But we've had people who took much longer than that."

"Drug trial? What drug trial?" I didn't take part in any drug trial.

"Oh, Anne, I'm so sorry to frighten you," Cynthia says quickly. "It really would be better for you if you came to meet us so that we can help you." Then she adds that I shouldn't worry about being whisked off anywhere by the government.

I wonder if she can read my mind! But I notice that she doesn't say I shouldn't worry about Esper whisking me off somewhere against my will. "Can I ask how old you are?"

I hang up.

I have a lot to think about. And worry about. What if I have zombiefied Melissa forever?

I'm still thinking about this as Gina and I get to work on my third epiphany.

"I can't believe you kept this a secret from me!" Gina says as we sit at her kitchen table with our laptops. "This is more unbelievable than Peaceflower being a guitar whiz! You're a real-life investor, not just for Theoretical Stockbroker club, and you don't even tell your best friend?"

"Well, it just sounds so—nerdy," I tell her. "I mean, I'm a fourteen-year-old girl. I shouldn't be spending all of my spare time working on my portfolio. I should be chasing boys and hitting the liquor cabinet, according to a report I heard on TV. I mean, can you imagine the headline, 'Teen Small-Time Investor'? It's just so boring."

I haven't told her about the ESP, because although she was a bit suspicious the other day, I don't want to worry her about me being able to possibly zombiefy someone.

"My God, Fiona, you're a dark horse," Brian says, and I freeze. I thought he was over at Joe's house tonight, but he has just sauntered in and is looking over his shoulder as if someone might be trailing him. "It's always the quiet ones you have to watch out for." If only Brian knew the truth! "Got any hot tips for us? Or any more dark secrets?"

"You *really* have your own portfolio?" Joe is, of course, with Brian. "I think that's *aymayzing*." His smile makes me go all Weak in the Presence of Beauty. But I am glad that I'm wearing the hipster jeans and pink T-shirt that Mum bought me, instead of my usual old jeans and a baggy top, because Joe Summers is looking at me in a very appreciative kind of way, which makes me feel a bit better.

"I wish my parents would let me use some of my savings to start my own portfolio, but they're worried I'd lose it." Joe is still looking at me in amazement (and appreciation).

"You would, mate, you're stock market crazy," Brian says. "So what are you worth, Ms. Blount? Enough to warrant a gigolo?"

"Actually she's a millionaire in Japanese yen," Gina tells them.

"My God, Blount, I think I'm in love." Brian dashes across the room and slides onto his knees in front of me and takes my hand, and I'm thinking, it's the wrong boy, even if Brian is only joking. "That's got to be—let me think—at least four thousand pounds!"

"I'm not telling," I say, batting my eyelashes back at him. "I am a woman of mystery." I cannot believe I just said that. I cannot believe what's come over me! It must be the worry and stress loosening my inhibitions.

And then Joe is on his knees in front of me, too, and takes my other hand, and I feel a little shiver go down my spine.

"A woman of beauty, intelligence, *and* mystery! Cast off this cheap gigolo and be mine, fair one. I love your blue-chip options. And your brain. Even though it is smaller than mine."

This makes me laugh even more, even though I wish it were true (the loving part).

Before I can stop myself, I say, "Question for you, Still You, because I am trying to establish whether boys are as intelligent as girls."

"Course we are," Joe says. "Smaller isn't always better," he adds, and I can feel my ears getting a bit pink again. Because I think he's flirting with me again! Flirting is much better than worrying about ESP!

"Okay," I say, because I'm obviously a mad, crazy woman. "You have to work out what the letters mean. If I were to say to you, thirteen L in a B D, what would be your answer?"

"Thirteen loaves in a baker's dozen?"

"Bingo!" Then I get all shy because I remember that Brian and Gina are both present, and Gina is giving me that knowing look again.

"She's a real-life Right Honorable, too, on account of her grandmother being a baroness," Gina says, then raises her hand to her mouth as she realizes what she has done. "Oops," she says, her eyes open wide with an unspoken "sorry."

See, this is why I haven't actually told Gina about my feelings for Joe. She means well, she really does, but every now and then these things kind of slip out of her mouth unintentionally. Can you imagine what would happen if the kids at school knew about the Right Honorable?

"You're kidding, right?" Brian asks.

"No," I say with a straight face, as I try to think of something that will diffuse the situation. "I really am a Right Honorable, one who has secret powers of ESP, and is also about to discover her long-lost millionaire father." This makes them laugh again, because it just sounds too preposterous to be true. And you know what? After all the stresses and strains of recent times, it feels so good to say it out loud and laugh.

"You had me at portfolio," Joe says, and for a moment, as I look into his lovely hazel eyes (which makes me feel so much like a cliché), I could almost believe him. I just really, really want him to like me. . . .

"Okay, lover boy," Brian interrupts as he gets to his feet, pulling Joe along with him. "Let's hit the bat cave. We have world domination to plan."

Joe lets go of my hand and gets to his feet, and I look away. To even imagine that he might like me is just so delusional.

"By the way," I say to him, "thanks for helping me out the other day in Mentoring Minds."

He pauses at the kitchen door. "Anytime."

As soon as they've gone back upstairs, Gina gets up and closes the kitchen door; then when she sits down, she takes my hands in hers. "You weren't joking about the ESP, were you?" she whispers.

I am speechless! How did she know?

Gina takes my silence as a yes. "I knew it! It's just like I said yesterday in the gym, isn't it? Now it all makes sense! Well, sort of."

"Okay," I say slowly, coming to a decision. "But you have to swear on everything sacred to you that you will never, ever tell a soul."

"I do," she says anxiously, squeezing my hands. "Because if the government ever found out, they'd whisk you away and I'd never see you again."

Gina's so perceptive about my secret fear! Plus, we watched *Phenomenon* together when it was on TV.

I take a deep breath and tell her about everything that has happened. Including the William Brown Talking Head part, and the Esper organization part. I don't even leave out the part where I might accidentally zombiefy someone. Like Melissa.

"I don't think you'd accidentally kill someone, though," she says calmly, when I have finished my tale. "What you have to do is to practice your powers on something small. Do you think you could, you know, make Kieran like me?"

The best thing about telling Gina is that she doesn't think I'm crazy. She's just taking it all in her stride, at face value, because she is my friend. And wondering how it all can benefit her, because I am hers.

"I don't know," I say morosely, thinking of Joe. And of Melissa, yesterday, and what Cynthia said. "I think messing with people's minds is probably not a good idea. Plus, it would be unethical."

"Yes, I thought that, too. Now," she says, all businesslike. "Let's get on with the plan."

We have written William Brown an e-mail (at the Info@ Funktech e-mail address), but with the cunning ploy of changing my last name from Blount to de Plessi (which is not an actual lie but is not the whole truth).

We have also used the cunning ploy of changing Gina's name, since she's my coconspirator in this plan. She's chosen the last name Roberts because that's Kieran's last name. "Even if it's only wishful thinking," she tells me as we read the e-mail one last time. "I definitely think Regina sounds more adult than Gina, don't you?"

"Absolutely. But do you think that William Brown will even bother replying?" I ask Gina anxiously. "I mean, he's a multimillionaire CEO and we are fourteen-year-old schoolgirls," I say, shaking my head.

"Fiona." Gina takes my hands and looks into my eyes. "Maybe he will, and maybe he won't. But you'll never find out if you don't try. Besides, remember—we're sixteen, now."

To: Info@Funktech.com
From: "Fiona de Plessi" <InvestorGirl@bluesky.com>
CC: "Regina Roberts" <InvestorGirl02@bluesky.com>
Subject: Investing in Funktech

For the attention of William Brown.
From: The Right Honorable Fiona de Plessi & Regina Roberts

Dear Mr. Brown,

Ms. Roberts and I are interested in investing two thousand pounds in Funktech. This is not a great deal of money to someone like you, but we are sixteen years old and everyone has to start somewhere. (Think of us as investors of the future!)

We've maintained our own stock portfolio for two years, and over this time we have increased our value tenfold.

Before we make a decision, we would like to arrange a meeting with you to discuss your company's admirable mission statement in closer detail, your views on industry and global warming, and the ethics

of your company in general (because we do not wish
to invest in a company that abuses its power, ruins
the environment, or mistreats any of its employees).

A little about Fiona de Plessi: I am part of my school's
Theoretical Stockbroker club, and it would be great
if you could find the time to give me some advice for
the club members. Additionally my relative, Baroness
de Plessi, maintains a much larger portfolio than I do,
and is always on the lookout for a good investment,
as are many of her friends.

A little about Regina Roberts: I am a reporter for
our school's newspaper and am writing a series of
columns titled, "Important Entrepreneurs of Our Time."
As a leading entrepreneur who came from humble
origins, you would be an inspiration for the younger
generation.

If you decide to grant us a little of your time, we are
available on Mondays and Fridays after 4 p.m., and
Tuesdays, Wednesdays, and Thursdays after 6 p.m.

We hope that we can meet with you.

Yours sincerely,

Fiona de Plessi
Regina Roberts

"Do you think I overdid it with Grandmother Elizabeth?"

"I think that your point about ethics and workers' rights was especially good because it's important that he knows his theoretical daughter has a conscience," Gina says. "You should use all the connections you have. This is going to be a total epic! I wonder how often he checks his e-mail?"

I don't point out to Gina that the e-mail address is generic, and that William Brown has loads of staff to check this kind of stuff for him. She's been so great about this whole ESP thing I don't want to, you know, make her feel silly.

"Um, I think we'll have to wait until at least Monday for a reply."

"Because anyone with a life will have a hot date on Saturday-hot-date night," Gina says, which makes me smile. She's so enthusiastic. But I think it's because she's thinking about Kieran, and how she'd like to have a hot date with him.

"Unlike us. And Joe." Which makes me think of Joe because I thought he was supposed to be hanging with Melissa Stevens (if she's not zombiefied) in Chaz Peterson's attic tonight. . . . Then I realize what I've said.

Gina looks at me in that strange way again. "Well, he wouldn't have a hot date tonight, would he?"

"Who hasn't got a hot date?" Joe asks as he walks into the kitchen and opens the refrigerator. "Because, you know, you only have to ask." Of course, I blush even more. Does he mean it? Is this flirting?

"Oh, Fiona's mysterious millionaire father." Gina says it with such a bland voice that it sounds completely improbable.

"Okay, okay." Joe laughs as he takes two cans of soda out

of the refrigerator. "I get it, private girl talk." If only he knew! Because if Joe had been two seconds earlier, he would have heard me. I must try to regain some of my Total Anonymity.

"So," Gina whispers the moment Joe leaves the room. "Is there something else you'd like to share with me?"

"No. It was just a comment, that's all. Because you know Melissa Stevens. She's not one to be left home alone on a Saturday night."

"Joe's not dating Melissa Stevens." Gina pauses, watching me carefully. "They broke up a few weeks ago, but Melissa wants to believe that he is still her boyfriend."

That is interesting.

"And you know what else? I think Joe likes you. You know—*likes you*, likes you."

If only that were true!

I really like Mark Collingridge, but he's not helping matters.

He's currently discussing *Minority Report*, which is a total disaster!

"Take it on down, bay—ay—bee, take it on down." Mum's voice carries down the hall from the kitchen (where she is cooking Sunday lunch for Mark Collingridge and me) into the living room, where I am supposed to be entertaining Mark Collingridge.

Up until now it's been pretty easy. Because all I have to do is ask him about a movie, and has he seen it? What did he think of it? Then off he goes! I mean, all I had to do was mention *Jerry Maguire* (because I love Renée Zellweger and this is one of my favorite movies). But instead of chatting about Renée he's giving me chapter and verse on Tom Cruise.

Which is how we got to *Minority Report*.

I haven't actually seen it, but I know all about it, now. It features three people who have the power of precognition, which means they can see the future, and are kept in custody by a nefarious scientific organization and the police, who exploit them to prevent crime. The three precognitives are drugged and asleep in a special tank all of the time, where they dream of crimes that have not yet been committed. Their dreams are captured on screen (in full color, apparently). They also dream the name of the future perpetrator, which is convenient for Tom Cruise (chief cop) and his team because they can prevent a crime from happening.

I mean, it's a neat story, but I don't want to be reminded of my ESP right now.

Mark Collingridge is just saying that "it's all about ethics," and I am thinking, absolutely it's unethical for the police to do that to those poor precognitives, then Mark Collingridge stops midsentence.

"Take it down down, take it down down," Mum sings, and I can tell that Mark Collingridge is in a world of his own. He's nodding along to the song and his hands are practically itching to play air guitar. It's quite sweet, actually. . . .

"Sorry, Fiona, I got a bit distracted," he tells me, and his face turns red. "Um, it's the music, it always carries me away. Where was I?"

"Don't worry." I take pity on him and pretend that I haven't noticed his embarrassment, especially because I know how it feels to worry about one's face giving away feelings when in the presence of or thinking of one's love. "I was a bit distracted myself there, too. Mum's such a great singer, isn't she?"

When I say that, Mark Collingridge goes even more red, if that's possible, so I quickly divert him by asking how the concert planning is going. He's been a tremendous help, according to Mum, because he knows so many people.

Mark Collingridge tells me about how his people are talking to Coldplay's people, and isn't it great how so many artists are actually donating their time for free, and I breathe a sigh of relief. I know that those three precognitives are only actors and pretending, but after the dreams I've been having I'm heavily invested in their well-being.

See, I had a weird dream the night before last. It started out nice, with Joe taking me out on a date. We were on some sort of roller coaster and he was telling me that he'd liked me for ages, and how much he loved that I was interested in science, and how Melissa Stevens was really an airhead but he was temporarily seduced by her beauty and blond hair. It was fabulous. But just as he was about to kiss me we were rudely interrupted . . .

It was William Brown Talking Head in my dream! He was *talking* to me. But I couldn't hear what he was saying to me.

I am even more afraid of what the future might bring.

Chapter 11

Wednesday's word of the day in Theory of Knowledge class: *parsimony*.

In science, it means a preference for the least complicated explanation for something (kind of what you have left once you have applied Occam's razor).

In life, it means taking extreme care to arrive at a course of action.

Like William Brown taking care to reply to two teenage girls! I mean it's only been four days now, which isn't much time, but I don't feel very hopeful.

Like my theory that I am parsimoniously fusing Total Anonymity, which seems to be working this week. Peaceflower hasn't, you know, done anything outrageous so far. Melissa has left us alone.

On the bright side, I don't seem to have done any permanent damage to Melissa, despite my unparsimonious use of

ESP on her last week. She's right back on form, as was obvious in homeroom when she and Suzy were holding court about how great it was on Saturday night in Chaz Peterson's attic, and what a shame it was that Joe couldn't make it because of other commitments and about who drank too much beer. I'm not a prude, but don't they know what an excess of alcohol can do to them? Not smart at all.

I am thinking all of this as Mr. Simpkins, our chemistry teacher who doubles as our Theory of Knowledge teacher, tells us about how we should take care when listening to a point of view and keep an open mind, and how we have to be parsimonious about how we come to a conclusion of who is right and who is wrong, and how sometimes there might not be a complete right or a complete wrong, when I get a severe case of prickles at the back of my neck.

As he is writing this quotation on the blackboard:

"Where there is shouting there is no true knowledge."
—*Leonardo da Vinci*

I just *know* that something bad is going to happen. After what Cynthia said to me about not knowing if I could accidentally damage someone's brain, I'm even more scared. I definitely don't want to do that!

I look first at Gina, who is sitting next to me, for signs of imminent danger, and she seems okay. So then I glance at Peaceflower, who is directly in front of me (because there was no spare seat next to Gina or me for this lesson), and she seems relatively danger free, too.

But the prickles get worse, and because I'm not thinking

clearly or doing a good job with Total Anonymity because of being totally freaked, I turn around to take a look at the rest of the class.

Of course, I am just in time to see Melissa throw a piece of chalk at Mr. Simpkins. The chalk lands right in the middle of the back of Mr. Simpkins's head with a dull thwacking sound, drops to his desk, then skitters onto the floor.

I can't believe she did that! I mean, maybe three years ago, but these days her form of torture is more subtle. You could hear a pin drop in the silence that follows.

And then, as you might expect, lots of kids start to laugh. I know that's mean, but it is kind of funny because it left a white mark in the middle of Mr. Simpkins's black, bushy hair. Plus, sometimes people laugh when they get to see something shocking (which this is) or when they are embarrassed (which I am for Mr. Simpkins). But I certainly do not laugh.

"Who did that?" Mr. Simpkins bellows, as he swings around. "Come on, who did it?" He is so angry and red faced. But then, who wouldn't be?

It has the effect of stopping all of the laughing because Mr. Simpkins is really big and tall, and has a thick black beard to go with his thick, bushy hair, and when he bellows he is a scary sight. Like Santa Claus's twin black-sheep brother.

"Okay, class, I am giving you exactly five seconds," he bellows again, "and if the culprit does not come forward, the whole of the class will receive a two-hour detention. Today. And you can bet that I will be there to make sure that you are all in attendance."

More bellowing from Mr. Simpkins is not helpful. So much for "Where there is shouting there is no true knowledge."

And thus begins my crisis of conscience (another one). To speak up, or not? Obviously my first instinct is to be invisible and keep my mouth shut.

"Five," Mr. Simpkins bellows.

And we all sit there just staring at him.

"Four—" he bellows again.

I really don't know what to do!

Tell him who did it? Which would make me a blabbermouth, and nobody likes a blabbermouth. Plus, it wouldn't exactly help with Total Anonymity fusion.

"Three—"

Then it happens, just as I am sure it will.

"You know, I hate to be a telltale, Mr. Simpkins, because that's just not my style," Melissa says in her saccharine voice. "But I don't see why the rest of us should be punished for the sake of one student. It was her." Melissa points at Gaynor Cole.

Then the whole of the class is looking at Gaynor with incredulity.

"What?" I can see that Mr. Simpkins doesn't really believe her, because you can tell from his tone of voice, and also by the astonishment written all over his face (despite his bushy beard).

"Er, I saw her do it, too." Suzy backs Melissa up.

Curiously Bev doesn't agree straightaway. Melissa looks across at her and inclines her head. "Yeah, it was her," Bev says. I'm a bit disappointed. Probably because we've been getting on quite well in Mentoring Minds. Yesterday she even told me about her grandma having a hip-joint operation, and how worried she was. I thought we were making progress.

"Gaynor, is that right?" Mr. Simpkins asks her in a much gentler tone. But it doesn't work, because Gaynor just sits there with her mouth wide-open and her shoulders drooping with defeat. *It's no good pushing her*, I want to say to Mr. Simpkins. That girl is much more scared of what would happen if she was to tell the truth.

As the silence around the room seems to go on forever, I can feel my blood beginning to boil because I'm angry, and what has Gaynor ever done to Melissa, anyway? And what did Melissa do to scare poor Gaynor last week when Peaceflower, Gina, and I had to take Gaynor to Mrs. Hunter? My face gets hotter, and before I can stop it the pressure starts to build in my brain. I start to see black spots again, and all I can think is, DO NOT let this HAPPEN. DO NOT let GAYNOR take the BLAME. I KNOW THE TRUTH and I CANNOT let her take the BLAME.

And as the buzzing in my ears gets louder, I WISH with all of my being that SOMEONE WILL TELL MR. SIMPKINS IT WASN'T REALLY GAYNOR. The pressure is so intense, I think I'm going to explode.

"Mr. Simpkins, Gaynor didn't do it," I blurt, releasing the pressure, and I want to faint as my brain seems to reverberate in my skull. I have a huge, instant headache! Gina's looking at me like I have gone completely mad. There are a lot of shocked gasps in that room. Including one from me, because I cannot believe what I have just done. I have just used my own compulsion power on myself! I want to be sick.

"Fiona, would you care to tell me who did do it?" Mr. Simpkins asks as Peaceflower turns around and stares at me with incredulity.

"Um." Not really.

My legs are shaking and my heart is pounding. What am I going to tell him?

"Fiona?" he prompts me again.

What do I do now? I swallow and try not to move my head very much.

"Um, it was. It was. It was. Me."

More collective gasps ensue, followed by silence as everyone waits to see what will happen next.

I can see that Mr. Simpkins doesn't really believe it was me, either, because he shakes his head and tells us all to read our textbooks quietly until the end of the lesson. Of course, he wants me to stay behind after class finishes (lunchtime) so that we can talk. The lesson seems to last for eternity. I mean, all I can do is worry about what is going to happen next. And how am I supposed to reachieve Total Anonymity fusion when I have just confessed in front of the whole class?

So it is a relief when the bell rings.

As Melissa leaves, she sidles up to me. "You're such a sucker, Mouse Girl. Have fun in detention!" She and Suzy laugh, but Bev doesn't even look at me.

"Don't worry about them, I think you're a true heroine," Gina whispers to me encouragingly, as she and Peaceflower gather their stuff. "You can, you know, stop them with your you-know-what." Then she twitches her nose like Samantha in *Bewitched*, and I'm thinking that she doesn't realize how tiring and difficult it is to use ESP.

Once everyone has gone Mr. Simpkins closes the door, and I think, *Now I am really in for it. I am in such trouble,* and my head is pounding so hard. Is he going to call my mother?

He walks across the room and stands right in front of my seat, but instead of looming at me from his great height, and instead of shouting at me, Mr. Simpkins sits down next to me.

"Fiona, I'm not an idiot. You're a good student. Let me make it clear that I do not believe for one instant that you threw that piece of chalk. I am right? Yes?" he says in a reasonable, almost a kindly, tone.

"Um. Yes." I mean, I cannot help but tell him the truth because I am (a) totally exhausted and (b) shocked that he is being nice to me.

"I am also assuming that you are worried about the repercussions if you were to tell me who really threw it."

"Yes," I say. I am also surprised that he has hit the nail so neatly on the head. Who knew that teachers could be so perceptive? "I would have to be parsimonious with the truth."

And then he nearly smiles (his mouth twitches under his beard). "All right. You've confessed to it, so I have to be seen punishing you. The detention stands, but I don't think we need to take it any further than that."

Whew. I grab my bag and head for the door. I can see why Ms. Maldine likes him.

"And Fiona," he says, just as I am about to open the door. I think, *What now?*

"That was a very noble thing you did."

"You are so brave! You are my heroine! Are you all right?" Gina is waiting for me outside the classroom with Peaceflower by her side. "Of course, I think you might be a bit mad, too. Total Anonymity, anyone? By the way, everyone knows it wasn't you who threw the chalk. But you're just so—so—

heroic!" Gina pats me on the arm in an understanding kind of way. Only she knows what I am going through! "Do you need two Tylenol?"

"I think I need more than that," I say wearily.

"Um, she didn't do it?" Peaceflower asks.

"Of course she didn't do it," Gina tells her, then adds loyally, "Fiona's far too nice to do something like that."

"I didn't think you really did it, but why confess to something you haven't done?" Peaceflower is confused. She is not alone.

"Fiona was being suicidal. And heroic." Surprisingly Mike is also waiting for me. "It was Melissa. I saw the whole thing. She's such a witch if she doesn't like you or doesn't get her own way. I should know." But I thought that in his role as Melissa's mentor she was treating him sweetly. I'm glad he's seen through her.

"Ahem." A quiet, timid person clears her throat. Gaynor Cole is also waiting for me, but standing a little bit apart from everyone else. "I, er, just wanted to say thank you," Gaynor says, blushing. "I don't know why you did it, though."

"You're welcome," I say glumly. Because apart from the fact that my head is splitting, I still have Melissa and Gang to worry about. Or at least Melissa and part Gang.

"What did Mr. Simpkins say to you? Are you in deep trouble?" Gina asks. "Did he suspend you?"

"He didn't believe it was really me, either. I just have to do the detention."

"But that's not fair!" Peaceflower is indignant on my behalf.

"Life isn't fair," I tell her, thinking of ESP and William Brown, and Melissa, and all the things I'd do if only I could get my ESP to work properly. How much simpler my life would be if William Brown 263 in my fact file turned out to be my father. He's a tax accountant who, according to his web page, likes to stay home and build miniature model airplanes during the week, and goes bird-watching at the weekends. Not terribly exciting, but at least I'd be more certain of a Predictable Routine if I were his daughter.

"Okay. 'Bye, and thanks again, it was really, um . . . nice of you," Gaynor says, and begins to shuffle off nervously down the corridor.

"Yeah," Mike nods morosely. "Well. To paraphrase the late, great journalist Edward R. Murrow, good-bye and good luck. You're going to need it."

If only he knew, I think as something else occurs to me. Mike and Gaynor are nice and if I am going to be whisked away by Esper to spend the rest of my life as a laboratory experiment at some point in the near future, then Gina and Peaceflower could use one or two more friends in their lives.

"Hey," I call after them. "Do you want to come and sit with us at lunch?"

Also, they really need to learn how to achieve Total Anonymity. Straight after I take two Tylenol and eat double calories, of course.

It would seem that everyone in the whole school knows what I have done.

Because as we go into the lunchroom, some students stop talking and nudge each other as I go past them.

"Well, here she is. Mouse Girl! With her loser friends," Melissa says, and she and Suzy burst into a fit of giggles. What a joke. Not. Suzy Langton's all, "Yeah, what a loser—taking the blame for something you haven't even done." Bev isn't smiling, though.

We walk to the fringes of the Clique Two crowd without saying a word. I just hope that Melissa will forget about us. I also hope that I'm going to get the low-level buzz in my brain back, so that I can re-fuse Total Anonymity. Cynthia was right when she said I wouldn't have energy to do anything after overextending!

"How are your grades, Melissa?" Andrea Spencer calls from her table with the tough kids by the wall. "Got all your As lined up for that Manhattan trip?"

I kind of wish I were more like Andrea. You know, not afraid of Melissa. Not afraid to stand out from the pack. Be different. I mean, Melissa usually doesn't bother Andrea.

"Shoo, fly." Melissa dismisses her with a flick of her hand.

"Make me," Andrea challenges her, and the Clique Three tough kids laugh. I can see Melissa doesn't like it much because she scowls and whispers something to Suzy and Bev.

But I am surprised when several people (who I don't even know) come up and say things like, "That was a really cool thing to do," and, "You're so brave," and, "It's about time somebody stood up to Melissa."

Even though my standing up to her is more passive resistance than actively standing up to her, it felt quite good. I feel even better after I've eaten my tuna sandwiches and high-calorie oat bars. Cynthia's advice about the calories was right, it would seem.

■ ■ ■

"By the way," Gina says as we leave class after the last bell has rung, "I'm coming to do detention with you."

"So am I," Peaceflower says.

"You guys are the best," I tell them, thinking at the same time how nice it is to have friends. I feel quite tearful with emotion.

When we arrive at the detention room, I get a bigger surprise. Gaynor and Mike are also there, even though we have only just become friends.

"Downtrodden of the School, unite." Mike holds up his fist in the air.

I am touched by this.

"Yes," Gaynor says nervously. "It's not much, just a little revolt against how unfair life can be. It doesn't change anything with the Melissa situation, but it's all we could think of."

I am speechless.

"What have we here?" Mr. Simpkins says as he strides into the room. "I wasn't aware of giving anybody else a detention tonight." But he is smiling.

"We're the Fiona Blount support group," Gina tells him solemnly. "Because she is a heroine."

"Can we join the Fiona Blount support group, too?" Joe asks as he, Kieran, and Brian hover in the doorway. I can't believe Joe deserted Melissa and Theoretical Stockbroker club to come to my detention. That's what I call karmic retribution!

"I told you, didn't I?" Gina leans across and murmurs in my ear as they come into the room and find a seat. She's blushing a bit, on account of her own True Love being present.

"Don't be silly," I say as Joe drags his chair in front of my desk, folds his arms on it, and rests his chin on his hands.

"Question, Marie Curie Girl," he says quite solemnly. "Five T on an F?"

"Answer, Still You," I say right back at him. "Five toes on a foot." And then we both laugh.

"You know what I mean," Gina whispers in my ear, and I try not to blush.

Maybe Joe really *does* like me, like me?

I hope I don't do something really awful with my ESP skills, like self-implode, before My Love for Joe can come to fruition.

Chapter 12

HINGS I WOULD DO WITH ESP IF POSSIBLE:

1. Persuade Joe to spend time with me, so that he can come to his own decision about whether or not he likes me.
2. Persuade Kieran to notice Gina, ditto above reason.
3. Persuade William Brown to meet with me.

What is Melissa up to?

Mike left our lunch table a few seconds ago because he has to print out some homework in the computer lab before the afternoon lessons begin. Melissa and Suzy have followed him and are talking to him by the door. It gives me a prickly feeling at the back of my neck, but they don't seem to be doing anything except talking to him, and he's staring at his shoes. Maybe it's the hard expression on Melissa's face that's making me suspicious.

"What are they doing? I mean, Mike's supposed to be

mentoring her, so she wouldn't be mean to him, right?" Gina asks.

"In theory. But you know Melissa. Maybe she's mad at him for sitting with us at lunch this week. Remember what he said the other day, about her being a witch." I just hope my fifteen minutes of fame ends soon. I can't tell you how difficult it is to be anonymous when people keep seeking me out to congratulate me on my courage.

I've been teaching Mike and Gaynor about Total Anonymity, too, because they need as much of it as they can get! Although I still don't know what's worrying them. I guess they just don't know us well enough to confide yet.

Melissa hands Mike a slip of paper. He blanches and leaves the lunchroom.

Melissa just laughs, then she and Suzy flounce back to their regular Clique One lunch table. It's a mystery! Mike will tell us when he's ready.

We still haven't heard from William Brown. And I haven't quite picked up the nerve to use the William Brown cell phone again. Instead, Gina has been helping me to work on my ESP. She says I owe it to myself to try because what good is a power if I can't use it at will? I've been using Peaceflower's crystal as a focus because that seems to help. Nearly.

I know that Cynthia said that I shouldn't try to use ESP for things (like using it on myself and possibly self-imploding), but I have to be able to control myself. Where's the harm in trying to get Peaceflower to blend in more? And why not try to make Kieran, you know, just notice Gina? Because if he did notice her, then the rest is up to him. And to Gina, of course.

"Are you doing it?" Gina whispers to me as I focus hard,

and she watches Kieran several tables away from us.

"Yes," I say to Gina between gritted teeth. I have Peaceflower's crystal in my hand (which is in my pocket) and I'm trying to re-create the feeling of how upset and mad I get when my ESP actually works. I think of how Melissa torments Gaynor Cole. And how she tried to hit Peaceflower with the tennis ball.

I'm concentrating so hard. . . .

Then it happens. I get that faint whisper in my ears, like radio static between two channels. Just as I get a very slight pressure in the base of my brain, Stephanie Gordon rushes across with some hot gossip for the Clique One girls. I'm struggling to hold on to the pressure, and also trying not to be distracted. How can Stephanie imagine that they'll make her a Clique One girl because of some gossip? Focus. Focus . . .

When Stephanie tells them, breathlessly, that Ms. Maldine has waxed off her mustache, I totally lose my concentration, just as Kieran glances over at us! Well, at Gina. Then he looks away again, but for a moment he really seemed to look at her.

"It worked!" Gina is euphoric. "Nearly. I mean he only looked at me for about a nanosecond, but it's a start."

I'm pretty euphoric, too, because surely Stephanie's news about Ms. Maldine is further proof of me conquering my ESP all by myself! Okay, so she didn't wax it off the same day I tried to plant the idea in her mind, but maybe it just took a little longer to sink in because I wasn't pushing with so much thought pressure.

"It did work, didn't it?" This is a breakthrough!

Then Stephanie Gordon totally bursts my ESP euphoria bubble.

Ms. Maldine's nonmustache has nothing to do with me, after all. Apparently a student from our school went onto a website called thetruthaboutteachers.com, where students can, you know, rate their teachers. This person wrote a comment about Ms. Maldine's hairy lip, and how she's really a man in disguise. Melissa and Suzy are, of course, laughing their heads off about it, but all I can think is poor Ms. Maldine!

Stephanie tells them that the kid in question was stupid enough to sign on with his own name. "Yeah, signing it Fat Mike was a dead giveaway." Suzy laughs and flicks her black curls over her shoulder. But when Chaz Peterson comments that she's not a bad teacher, and why would someone sign their own name? Suzy just tells him he's being an idiot. Bev's not saying anything at all. Melissa definitely shouldn't be so happy about it, though. . . .

"Poor Mike." Gina shakes her head. "This is so obviously a setup."

"He's smart. And nice. He wouldn't write that about Ms. Maldine." Why would someone want to do this to him?

"I'm going to keep my ear to the ground, because this sounds like a possible story for the school paper." Gina looks across at Kieran as she says this. "It would be a great scoop. Maybe you could, you know, help?" Gina wrinkles her nose in the manner of Samantha. If all I had to do was wrinkle my nose, I'd be ESPing all over the place!

Then I have another thought. What if, somehow, I really did cause Ms. Maldine to wax her mustache, but inadvertently instead of directly? What if I made a mistake while I was trying to project my thought into Ms. Maldine's brain, and accidentally put the thought into someone else's mind? Which caused them to write that message on thetruthaboutteachers.com?

I am still thinking about this when I arrive at Mentoring Minds. Ms. Maldine's eyes are red, and she's not booming very much. Mr. Simpkins is trying to cheer her up with a book about Tim Henman, Ms. Maldine's supreme tennis hero. Mr. Simpkins says that it sheds unique light on Tim and the Henmania that sweeps the nation whenever Tim strides onto a tennis court. But she only musters up a half smile.

I shake my head as I walk across the room and sit next to Bev. I am *so* not in the mood for her today. See, it's occurred to me that maybe I put that waxing thought about Ms. Maldine into Bev's mind! How can I mentor someone who has possibly done something like that? She is predisposed to bullydom, after all.

I don't look at her as I take out my textbook. But I do look at Mike, who has just entered the library. Everybody's looking at him, and there's a low murmur of speculation and gossip. But I think how brave he is—despite everything he's here to mentor Twit Melissa—Ms. Maldine *must* realize that message had nothing to do with him!

"Mike," Ms. Maldine says, and her voice is a little more boomlike. "I know that you'd never do anything like that, you are as much a victim in this as, well . . ." Ms. Maldine peters out and I can see the whole waxed-lip thing is really embarrassing her.

I catch his eye as he takes his place next to Melissa and give him a thumbs-up for solidarity, and Mike kind of nods. After all, maybe his predicament was all my fault in the first place. Then I turn my head and Joe is watching me, and he smiles, so I smile back. This gives me courage.

"Okay," I say as I open my math textbook. "Quadratic equations. Here," I say, pointing to an equation, "a, b, and c are coefficients—"

Bev interrupts me. "That fat kid, he's a friend of yours?"

"Yes," I say simply. Which is not a lie, but is not the whole truth. Yet.

"Well, that thetruthaboutteachers.com thing wasn't anything to do with me. Get it? That thing about guitar girl, that was just a friendly warning. Not a threat from *me*. Get it?"

"I get it," I tell her, even though I don't. Maybe I'm wrong about leaking thoughts, too. But what if it's possible?

I don't get my ESP, either.

"Hostelier to His Highness, The Prince of Wales," Gina sighs. "Do you think you could, you know"—Gina wrinkles her nose at me, as we gaze up at the magnificence that is the Ritz Hotel—"imagine a booking for us? I've always wanted to have afternoon tea here."

"I really owe you one for being such a good friend," I say because it's true. She's been so supportive of me in this quest. "But I think that would be fraud," I add as I get the William Brown mobile phone out of my bag.

"Not if we paid for it, it wouldn't be."

"Small problem." I grin at her. "It's thirty-six pounds per person. So unless you carry seventy-two pounds around with you as a matter of course, we're out of luck. Next time."

"Oh. Sorry," she says, patting my shoulder. "You're concentrating."

I need to ring the William Brown Talking Head mobile phone again, to check out my theory of leaking thoughts and the damage they might do to others! Gina says I should definitely get more answers, anyway, because I need as much information as I can get my hands on, and as my friend she insisted on coming with me. Besides, The Ritz was her idea because it is the poshest of posh hotels, and royalty come here. I thought it was brilliant of her to suggest it, because it ties in nicely with the royal connection and satellite tracking of phones.

"Okay. Are you ready, Fiona?"

"I'm ready."

"That's good. Now make that call, and make sure you ask for the actual William Brown."

I try to control my rapid breathing as I ring the number. What if William Brown answers it himself this time? But he doesn't, of course. I get Cynthia again.

William Brown isn't available, but Cynthia goes to great lengths to tell me how sorry she was to scare me, and how happy she is that I've not cut off contact, and that I can feel free to ask her anything I need to know. So I ask her what she meant about the drug trial during our first conversation, because it's been worrying me.

"I took part in a trial for a new drug nineteen years ago," Cynthia tells me slowly. "At first, I was fine, but some time later I developed abilities that other people don't have. I thought I was going crazy until Esper contacted me."

"Esper found you?" I squeak. "Did they find you using their ESP skills?" I'm wondering if the William Brown Talking Head in my dream the other night was William Brown really trying to make contact with me after that incident outside

Westminster Abbey. I haven't heard from him again, which is a relief, but you never know with this ESP stuff.

"No, please don't be alarmed, Anne," Cynthia says soothingly. "It wasn't like that. The founders of Esper obtained a list of all the people who'd taken part in the trial and wrote to them. In the letter was a message that only people with our abilities could see. Once I got over my initial shock, I got in touch with Esper, and I've been part of the organization since then. It's really helped me," Cynthia says.

"Do, um, other people develop skills? I mean, people who didn't take part in the trial?" I ask because I'm thinking that I must have inherited mine from William Brown.

"None currently. All our espees took part in the drug trial. Of course, the exceptions are their children, who inherit the abilities. Anne, you don't sound old enough to have taken part in the trial, so I'm assuming one of your parents did. Have you confided in either of them about your skills?"

This spooks me because I don't want to go into my possible William Brown parentage. Instead I ask her if it's possible that I've been using ESP for low-key things like Total Anonymity for years, without even realizing it. When I tell her how it feels, she tells me that I've got it right, which really helps.

When I also explain about trying to concentrate on doing simple ESP things when I'm not angry or afraid by using the crystal as a focus, she tells me that they're one of the objects Esper uses as a training aid. So far so good.

"But is it possible to, you know, accidentally leak thoughts into the wrong people's heads?" She doesn't answer me straightaway.

"It's a possibility," she says, and I think she's hedging. Everything's a possibility!

"That doesn't really tell me very much."

"Our scientists are still accumulating knowledge about our powers and testing how they work."

Scientific testing? I mean, I approve under normal circumstances, but not if it's *me* being scientifically tested. I hang up.

"Well?" Gina asks me, concern written all over her face.

"She mentioned scientists and testing."

"That would spook me, too," she says. "We should keep an open but wary mind about Esper until we have more information because I don't want you to be whisked away forever!"

I'm beginning to think that I'll never see William Brown. Unless he decides to sponsor the charity concert. His Talking Head seems nice but I think I'd feel a lot better about this whole thing if I could just meet him and decide for myself.

On my way to Theoretical Stockbroker club, I am wondering about how to meet him and how I can furtively check out Funktech's sponsorship with Sharon, when I get my next shock.

What is Andrea Spencer doing in Theoretical Stockbroker club? Especially as she can't stand Melissa. I didn't think she was a joiner. I guess she's after SACS points, too. There she is, clear as day, chatting to Nigel Corrie about an embezzlement scandal in today's newspaper.

Melissa is scowling across at Andrea, but Andrea seems to be oblivious to her. Then Joe introduces his proposal for investment. I mean, I thought he was joking when he sent it to all the stockbrokers via e-mail last night.

But he's serious! I don't understand how Joe, who is usually a genius (a hot-guy one), can think that this is a good idea. All it takes is a small amount of research on the Internet about Holwell Holdings to discover that the people running it are a bunch of crooks! It's owned by Morris Thornwell, who is suspected of being in charge of local organized crime.

"So." Joe smiles at us when he finishes his presentation, and my heart does a flippy thing in my chest. "Shall we put it to the vote?"

"I trust you, Joe!" Melissa Stevens jumps straight in. "I vote yes." Of course she does. I can't believe I ever thought she was fairly smart.

Of course Suzy Langton and Chaz Peterson vote yes, too. Nicholas Bergin and Luiz Harani don't feel strongly either way, and Harry Emond thinks we should do some more research before we decide. Peaceflower's new crush, Buzz, just says, "Whatever you think, man." Well, the guy's obviously a musical genius. I guess he can't be good at everything.

I instinctively glance sideways at Mike, and he raises his eyebrows at me. A fellow doubter! Nigel Corrie obviously doesn't like the idea either, because he's scowling and frowning at the finance report. Then I make the mistake of glancing around the circle and accidentally meet Andrea's gaze. She rolls her eyes at me.

"Andrea, how about you?" Joe asks. "What do you think?"

"That company has bad karma, man. Not a sound investment." Andrea shakes her head. "Morris Thornwell has a history when it comes to owning companies. His last one went bankrupt."

Exactly!

Melissa Stevens obviously cannot bear to have the love of her life (even if he is no longer) criticized. "Don't you think that Joe did his homework on this? Anyway, there are eleven of us, and you're the only one who's spoken out against it. You lose."

"Oi, pretty girl. Some of us have brains and did our homework before the meeting," Andrea tells her, and I think again how brave she is.

"Melissa." Joe holds up his hands. "Andrea made some good points. And we haven't heard from everyone else yet. Nigel? Mike? Fiona?"

To agree, or not to agree, that is the question. Will Melissa find ways to torture me if I don't? Will Joe hate me if I do not go with his flow? But Joe also knows about my secret portfolio, therefore must assume that I am fairly good at researching my investments. . . . Mike and I look at each other. I think about his bravery with the Ms. Maldine incident, and before I can stop myself, I blurt, "I agree with Andrea."

"Yeah." Mike nods mournfully. "She's right about Thornwell. He's been arrested twice on suspicion of laundering money, but the police couldn't find any evidence."

"And the rest of it. Assault, dodgy deals," Andrea says, glancing at Mike and me. "I've got a lot more stuff in here." She holds up a folder.

"I missed the assault charges." I surprise myself by actually speaking to her. I hold up my own folder.

"His last company went bankrupt under very suspicious circumstances, with thousands of pounds of overseas investments disappearing," Nigel says, and frowns even more at the financial report.

"There's just so much about him online." Andrea grins at us. "If I'd printed it all off it would have taken a rain forest of trees."

"When you four have finished bonding"—Melissa jumps back in—"I still say we go with Joe's gut feeling."

"Yes, because it's always better to trust your gut feeling than look at the evidence," Andrea says, and I nearly laugh at the sarcasm in her voice.

Everyone except Melissa votes against Joe's proposal. Even Joe doesn't vote for his own proposal. And thus the meeting is closed, and I cannot believe that for a moment there Andrea seemed to be quite an accessible human being.

As I watch Melissa fawn all over Joe from the corner of my eye, my hand slips around the crystal in my pocket. And as Joe tries to extricate himself from her, I squeeze on it. I wonder about Joe liking me. As I feel the faint pressure in my brain, instead of thinking about not being noticed—I can't help it—I wish, just a little bit, that Joe would, you know, notice me and want to spend a bit of time with me. What's the harm in that?

I totally lose concentration when someone talks to me. "Cheers for supporting me on that," Andrea says, and I'm totally confused. Can I just say that I am finding my position of being on the same side as her pretty weird? "I was a bit nervous about contradicting Joe," she continues, "because his proposals are usually watertight. The man has a brain."

"Yes." I nod.

"And he's easy on the eyes," she adds, grinning at me, and I can't help it, I grin back.

"Yes."

And then we remember our respective places in the school hierarchy, and it feels awkward again. Weird.

It doesn't look as if that teeny Joe thought worked, either, because he's engrossed in conversation with Melissa. What if he's thinking of reuniting with her?

Five minutes later, as I walk down Kingsway, I get another surprise. I hear a voice behind me.

"Hey, Fiona, wait." It's Joe. Oh. My. God.

"Hi," I say as he walks up to me. Of course, every coherent thought flies out of my head, except that Joe is here with me, and did I do this with my ESP?

"Question, Marie Curie Girl," he begins, and my heart races even faster. I am getting to like this particular game.

"Fire away, Still You." I really love that he calls me Marie Curie Girl!

"Mind if I walk with you? I think you live on Royal Crescent? I'm just around the corner on Ladbroke Grove."

That is definitely not the question I was expecting. And I am confused. Is he walking with me because I am here, or because he wants to walk with *me* in particular?

Of course, I already know where he lives, but I can't believe he knows which road I live on. My heart is pounding so hard it is a wonder that he cannot hear it.

"Um. Yes. It's a free sidewalk," I say. His smile slips a little as if I only agreed that he could walk with me because of the sidewalk being free.

For what feels like an eternity (but in reality is only a few seconds), we walk in silence, and I know that I should say something.

"Um, I'm sorry for what happened back there."

"Are you kidding? It was a setup. I wanted to see if anybody really had researched anything other than last year's finance report and the stock prices."

"No!" I laugh. "That was devious."

"Well, it worked. And it's given everyone something to think about." Then he adds, "I knew I could depend on you to, you know, cut my manly brain down to size," but in a joking way, which makes me laugh again.

"Someone has to keep you in your place."

"You're doing a fine job, Marie Curie Girl," he says, and nudges his arm against my shoulder (on account of his shoulder being quite a bit higher than mine). It sends little shivers down my spine.

What do I say to him now? I so want to make a good impression, but I hardly talk to girls, let alone boys. Joe, thankfully, breaks the silence. "What do you do for fun when you're not taking over the financial world, or being a Right Honorable?"

If only he knew!

"Oh, you know." I shrug. "All the usual stuff."

"Like reading up on quantum mechanics and cosmology?"

"Yeah, I know that's weird," I say because it is. Even more weird is (a) finding my secret millionaire father, and (b) testing my ESP! Joe will think I'm an idiot. I put my hand in my pocket and grasp my crystal for moral support.

"No, definitely not weird," Joe says, smiling down at me. "Definitely not weird. Besides, my mother's a cell biologist—she worked on the Human Genome Project—and my father's a quantum physicist. Can you just imagine the conversations in my house? While Mum's going on about the base of the most common nucleotides, Dad's talking about the possibility of multiverses. So, you see, by comparison you're totally normal."

Joe thinks I'm not weird! "So, um, what do you do when you're not doing quantum stuff with your dad, and conquering the cyber world with Brian?"

"Oh, I'm pretty quiet. Pretty boring, mostly," he says, which I am sure is not true. And then he grins at me. "Want to get a boring soda?"

"Sorry?" For a moment I don't get his meaning. He's asking me if I want to get a soda from the fast food place we are passing? Me?

"I could drink a soda, boring or otherwise," I say, smiling. I shrug, just to let him know that it is no big deal, and that I am not misunderstanding that this is a date or anything.

"Good, because I want to hear all about your"—he pauses as he pushes the door open, and waits for me to go through—"stock options."

"Okay," I say, wondering if maybe this is a date.

Of course, soda with Joe is not boring at all. First, he insists on buying my soda because he says it's only fair after I saw through his bogus investment plan. Then he chooses a secluded booth in the corner of the café, and it feels even more like a date! Seclusion, so that we can, you know, talk. Only thing is, I don't know what to talk about. But Joe saves me from that.

"Okay, a challenge for you. Three questions each; winner buys the sodas next time. What do you say?" he asks me as we sip our drinks.

Next time? Does he mean the next drink now, or next time we come for a drink together?

"It's a deal," I say, and I concentrate on my soda so he cannot see the redness of my cheeks. "Gentlemen first," I add, and when I peek at him, he flashes me that enigmatic smile.

"Okay, here we go. Number one. Twenty-six L of the A."

"Twenty-six letters of the alphabet." That was obvious—I think he's being easy on me.

"Beginner's luck," he says, shaking his head. But when I guess his second question, which is 90 D in a R A (obviously 90 degrees in a right angle), he laughs, and my heart does that flippy thing, because he's so cute, and I'm thinking this *really is flirting.* "I'm going to have to find a tougher one for you. Okay, nine P in S A." Then he leans back in his seat and folds his arms on the table.

"Um," and I am thinking that it's 9 Provinces in South Africa, but I don't want to appear too smart, because that can put boys off. Plus, even if Joe guesses my three questions, this will mean that if I lose, I get to buy him a soda next time, which means there will actually be a next time.

"Got you." He laughs. "Go on, admit it."

If only he knew how much he's got me. But I can't say that. Instead, I tell him my first question, which is 9 L of a C. Which he gets straightaway is 9 lives of a cat, and rubs his hands together, and I'm thinking how cute that flip of his hair is. And how his eyes are like caramel mixed with pale, creamy swirls of honey. And when I ask him, 32 is the T in D F at which W F, he totally gets that it's 32 is the temperature in degrees Fahrenheit at which water freezes. When he guesses my third one, which is 1,000 years in a millennium, I tell him that next time, the sodas are definitely on me, and he grins and says absolutely.

But when we walk as far as our routes home take us, he doesn't, you know, say anything about an actual date for the next soda. He just says, "See you."

Obviously the ESP suggestion has worn off.

But I do want him to love me for myself, not because I've forced him.

Chapter 13

I can't believe I'm going to meet my possible-very-probable father! In an hour's time!

There was an e-mail waiting for me in my inbox when I arrived home last week after my nonboring soda with Joe. It's kind of like Joe is a good-luck charm for me. Okay, it wasn't actually from William Brown, but it was from his assistant to inform Gina and me that Mr. Brown had a small window of opportunity to speak with us. His assistant indicated that William Brown is usually booked up far in advance and if we couldn't make this appointment we might have to wait for weeks. So, of course, I e-mailed back right away to accept.

I've been a total bag of nerves and excitement ever since, because what if I don't like him? Even worse, what if William Brown doesn't like me?

I also can't believe that the nine days since I got the e-mail about the appointment could rush by so swiftly, because I thought they'd drag, but they haven't. There's just been so much happening.

Last Saturday morning, when I explained to Mum about Gina and me interviewing captains of industry for a series of articles Gina's doing for the school paper (which is not a lie, but is not the whole truth, because we're only interviewing *one* captain of industry), and what did Mum think would be the appropriate clothes to wear? And how should we wear our hair? Well, she immediately decided that it was time for a bit of her favorite retail therapy. I think she was just excited that I was showing a real interest in clothes for a change.

A girl (and her best friend) has to look as good as possible for her first meeting with her probable father, doesn't she? I mean, I have to make an effort.

Also, Mum's been so busy working on the concert plans, and practicing with the Bliss Babes, and dating Mark Collingridge, I think she was feeling a bit guilty about not having spent much time with me recently. But Madonna has been so great about endorsing the concert (she even signed the promotion letters that went out to the possible sponsors), Mum deserves some time out.

After a quick phone call to Gina, and to Mum's friend and hairstylist Gustav, who said that he'd be happy to fit us in as a favor to Mum (and also because of the free CDs she gives to him), she hustled us to Oxford Street to find outfits for us. I have to say that Mum has impeccable taste in clothes. I got a silver-gray sort of crinkled skirt with a stylish cropped jacket, which I think is very simple yet elegant, but not too old for me. Gina got a black ruffled satiny skirt and a black fitted jacket. We both got stylish low-heeled black pumps to complete the outfits. Mum says that you can't go wrong with black and neutral colors for business.

When we went for our hair appointments, we told Gustav that we needed something that wasn't drastic, something flexible—you know, something that wouldn't be outrageous for school (especially because of Total Anonymity), but that could be made into something more glamorous out of school—he came up with the perfect styles for us. Mine is cropped to neck length and a bit spiky and flicky, but can still be tied back for school. Gina's is still long and auburn, but Gustav cut off about five inches and did something to it so it's all silky and curves under. Plus the bangs really suit her.

We went back to my house and tried on our outfits with our new hair, and while Mum got ready for her date with Mark Collingridge she said we should try a little bit of neutral makeup to finish the effect. Just a little bit of blush and some clear lip gloss.

Mark Collingridge thought we looked lovely, then told us all about the movie *She's All That*, and how gorgeous swans are often hidden behind ugly-duckling facades, and then went on to tell us the plot of the story even though Gina and me have seen it about a million times.

Did he just insult us (by calling us ugly ducklings) or compliment us (gorgeous swans)?

In any case, when he saw Mum in her new outfit, a black leather skirt and black V-neck top, his eyes nearly popped out of his head, and he told her that she was a babe. That kind of worried me because Mark Collingridge seems to be getting very attached to Mum. I mean, I'm about to meet my probable father! Mum's long-lost love! What if it really does create a love triangle?

I told Gina about my worries, and she said that I am totally doing the right thing because every girl has a right to meet her own father. And find out about her ESP, of course.

I feel I've been getting more of an idea of how to control the low-level ESP pressure for Total Anonymity this week. I've been trying to expand it to make it stronger, without having to get too emotional. First, I imagine the low-level pressure as a bubble in my brain, then I make myself just a little bit more fearful (only a little) and use that fear to expand the bubble to encompass me, then my friends as well. Kind of like a bubble of invisibility.

This seems to be harmless to others and beneficial to Gina, Peaceflower, Gaynor, Mike, and me, especially for those Melissa moments at lunchtime. I haven't really tried to do anything else because what if I cause something major to happen and there are unexpected consequences *à la* zombiefying of Melissa?

Okay, so on Monday in geography, when Miss Ethelridge asked if someone could point out Reykjavik on the map of the world, I panicked a bit, because Peaceflower put up her arm. I had my hand on the crystal at the time, and I was thinking about another idea I'd had—to imagine my thoughts as a beam of light emitting from the crystal and into the mind of the person I was trying to affect—and I thought, *Don't let Miss Ethelridge see Peaceflower's arm.*

Then it happened. *Poof!* I felt a slight whoosh as the thought left my brain. Not like the pressure I feel when I'm accidentally doing something major, though. But it worked! Miss Ethelridge chose Harry Emond to answer the question instead. Honestly I worry about what will happen to Peaceflower if I'm not around, I really do. But when I reminded her about Total Anonymity at lunch, Peaceflower was really, like, so sorry about being such a scatterbrain that I felt bad about mentioning it. She has to learn somehow.

But what a breakthrough!

Okay, so it happened again on Tuesday, too, in the computer lab, when Gina and I were composing our questions for William Brown. We were sitting behind Kieran, and we could see he was working on something for the latest edition of the newspaper. I'd been trying all week without success to re-create the beam-of-light feeling I'd had in geography, and I really wanted to do something nice for Gina, so I tried it on Kieran. Then it happened again!

He turned around and spoke to us! He asked us what we thought of the current edition of the newspaper. I told him it was fantastic, and that I particularly enjoyed Gina's article about the environment, and then I encouraged Gina to tell him about her latest idea of including a wacky horoscope. He and Gina chatted about it very enthusiastically, and it made me happy to see her making progress with the man of her dreams!

Then Melissa, Suzy, and Bev totally ruined the moment when they came in to do some last-minute English homework Melissa had forgotten about. Of course, because we were talking to Kieran they noticed us instantly. They didn't say anything to us on account of Kieran being there, but Melissa and Suzy were all over him like a rash. Bev wasn't so enthusiastic, though. She kind of kept looking at me in a strange way.

In Mentoring Minds after school on Thursday, Bev was really quiet. I was thinking about Melissa, and why she does the horrible things she does, at the same time that I was explaining to Bev that the "solutions" of quadratic equations are also the x intercepts on the graph. Bev put down her pencil.

"She's not a totally bad person, you know," she said, and I nearly fell off my chair. Was I emitting my thoughts again? "She has a hard time at home. Get it? Her dad has really high expectations of her, and her mother's more interested in what Melissa looks like than her daughter's life. And things haven't been going her way with certain people."

"Oh." I couldn't think of anything to say. Did she mean Joe in that last part? I thought Bev was going to say something more about it because she opened her mouth. But she closed it again, picked up her pencil, and refocused on the equations.

I could have used a bit of ESP on Wednesday at Theoretical Stockbroker club, too, because it was my turn to do a presentation, and what if they all thought I was an idiot? You know, I really wanted them to approve of an investment in Funktech. Not just because of the William Brown connection, but because it really is a good investment. I just kept thinking, *This is such a great company.*

It didn't really work that time, though, because (of course) Melissa, Suzy, and Chaz didn't think it was a good idea. That is, until Joe, Nigel, and Andrea said they thought it was brilliant. It was totally weird having Andrea approve of me again, I can tell you, but she kept going on about what a wonderful discovery Funktech was. Melissa didn't like that very much, but because Joe approved, she changed her vote. I thought about what Bev had said, and to be honest, I felt a bit sorry for Melissa. I know how unrequited love feels!

Although I might just have used a little bit of ESP on Joe

afterward, too—not enough to make him love me or any-thing—just a suggestion that he'd walk home with me again. I definitely felt a slight whoosh as I looked at him, but I'm not sure if I accidentally emitted a love vibe. I definitely didn't think anything about sodas. But he suggested it again—right in front of Melissa! Well, of course I said yes, even though she was glaring at me at the time. I just didn't feel as nervous of her as I usually do. I mean, should I reject my One True Love just because of Melissa?

So we did—go for soda, I mean, and we played the guess-ing game again. Afterward, he told me he was having a hard time with Kieran in Mentoring Minds and, before I could stop myself, I told him that maybe his explanations were too complicated.

"You think?" he asked, like he was really taking in what I said.

"Well, yeah," I said. Then I suggested that he use an anal-ogy. "Okay, take three people. One speaks only French, i.e., DNA. One speaks only English, i.e., the amino acids that build proteins. The third speaks English and French, i.e., RNA, therefore it can translate instructions from DNA to the amino acids."

I was worried that I might have hurt his ego or something, so it was a surprise when Joe grabbed me by the shoulders and kissed me on the cheek.

"You're brilliant," he said. I blushed and looked down at my soda, because I didn't know what to say. Did he mean I was brilliant in a romantic kind of way?

I was still daydreaming about that moment this morning in the chaos that is English, and getting nervous and excited about my meeting with William Brown tonight, when I did something stupid. I forgot about Total Anonymity. While Ms. Woods was trying to explain about the use of metaphor as she handed out our marked papers on *Great Expectations* (which in my opinion should be retitled *Don't Expect Great Expectations*), Melissa let out a squeak of indignation, because she'd gotten a C.

"This is so not fair," I heard her tell Suzy and Bev. Which was kind of hard due to the noise levels in the class, but from the fringe of Clique Two where Gina, Peaceflower, and I were sitting, as usual, I could just make out what she was saying. "I *can't* let my grades slip, I just *can't*. I've been getting straight As in English since the beginning of this half term! This will, like, totally kill my chances of that Manhattan trip!"

"But I thought that fat nerd was doing your English—" Suzy cut off, and I wondered what she was going to say next. Then I got the familiar prickle at the back of my neck. I should have been more scared, but I wasn't. Possibly because all of my emotions were being taken up due to (a) fear, anxiety, and excitement for my meeting with William Brown, and (b) my love for Joe. But I knew something was going to happen.

I turned around just in time to see Melissa fold a piece of paper and pass it to Suzy. I froze, because Melissa looked up and I accidentally made eye contact with her! She kind of smirked at me. Suzy passed the note to the student in front of her, and so it went on until the last kid—Harry Emond, in Clique Four—handed it to Ms. Woods.

When Ms. Woods opened it, her face fell. I could see tears in her eyes! It was obvious that the note wasn't very nice, because Ms. Woods scurried out of the classroom like a frightened mouse.

Melissa and Suzy were laughing their heads off. Until Mr. Simpkins loomed through the door with that piece of paper in his hand. Of course, Mr. Simpkins demanded to know where the note had come from, else we'd all be in detention after school. Which would have been a disaster because Gina and I would have missed our meeting with William Brown!

This time, when Suzy said that she hated being a blabbermouth but Mike had written the note, it was obvious that nobody believed it. Of course, when Melissa backed her up, nobody believed that, either. Melissa nudged Bev, but she didn't say a word. She just sat there looking miserable. Poor Mike looked pretty miserable, too. First the online smear, and now this!

I just *knew* what was going to happen; it was history repeating!

So I confessed. I didn't even compel myself this time. I couldn't believe it!

Mr. Simpkins handed me the note and asked me if I was sure. Let's just say that the whole class was hanging on every word. The note was pretty mean—it was a poem.

> *ROSES ARE RED,*
> *VIOLETS ARE BLUE,*
> *SPIDERS ARE UGLY,*
> *AND SO ARE YOU!*

All in block capitals, so it was hard to compare the handwriting. I felt terrible for Ms. Woods.

"Um, yes, it was me," I said, even though I hated speaking in front of everyone. "Um, but it wasn't for Ms. Woods," I told him, thinking on my feet. "I had a problem with someone, and I wrote that poem to, you know, make myself feel better.

I didn't intend to give it to anybody. And I certainly didn't pass it along to Ms. Woods. I didn't even touch the paper on its way to the front. So somebody must have taken the poem from among my things—you know, maybe in physical ed, because you can't keep an eye on your things all of the time in physical ed—and taken it for their own nefarious reasons."

After I said all of that I felt awful. I'd lied. All because of Melissa. If only I'd had the courage to tell him the real truth. Mr. Simpkins was nice about it, and when I told him that I'd do the detention but could we delay it until next week on account of me having unavoidable plans after school, he was really understanding. So was Ms. Woods when I repeated it to her and apologized. She just patted my hand and said of course I hadn't meant it about her, because she knew I wasn't that kind of person.

By lunchtime, everyone seemed to know, so Total Anonymity was impossible for the rest of the day. Just like the time before, everyone kept coming up to me and con- gratulating me on my bravery. Melissa and Suzy glared at me all through lunchtime, but with so much attention on me they didn't dare try anything.

After our last class, Gina and I rushed to her house. We've spent the last hour trying to re-create our "look" from our visit with Gustav for our meeting with William Brown. See, since she lives much closer to the Underground than I do, we don't have very far to walk in our heels. I'm getting butterflies in my stomach. What if William Brown doesn't like me? What if I don't like William Brown?

"Stop worrying." Gina nudges me and smiles at me in the mirror as she strokes blush on her cheeks. "He'll love you." I may be the one with ESP, but it seems like Gina's the mind reader.

We spent hours agonizing over the questions we're going to ask William Brown. All the obvious ones, of course, about his career, but also carefully worded, personal ones to, you know, establish if he is my William Brown or not. However, I definitely thought, "Did you have a pet dog when you were younger, and what was it called?" might be a bit too suspicious.

But we've included the one about why he chose to expand Funktech to Britain, and when was the first time he visited Britain (because I remember Mum saying that when she met him it was his first trip).

Gina takes my hands. "Are you ready?" she asks, her expression serious.

"Yes. I am." Although I'm completely scared.

"Oh," Gina says as she opens her nightstand drawer and takes out a small vial. "This is just in case we get the chance to steal one of his hairs. For DNA testing."

As we walk down the stairs, I'm thinking for the thousandth time since all this craziness began what a great friend she really is. "We can't just pull a hair out of his head, though," I tell her.

"I didn't mean we should do that," she says as we reach the bottom. "I meant that if I happen to see one on his jacket, or something, I could surreptitiously sneak it. Because DNA testing is the only way you're going to—" She pauses, and I nearly collide with her.

Joe's standing there in the hallway, with a sandwich on his plate. And with his mouth wide-open. His eyes are wide-open, too. I thought we had the house to ourselves. Mrs. Duffy is at work, and I thought Brian and Joe were at Joe's house.

"Wow." He looks at us both in what I think is a shocked kind of way. But a good shocked. And particularly at me. "Nice, um, clothes."

I go all warm inside. "Um, thanks," I say, aiming for maximum facial inscrutability. I am also wondering if he heard Gina's remark about the DNA test.

"My God, who are these stunning creatures?" Brian whistles as he comes out of the kitchen and puts his hand on his heart. "Well, stunning creature *singular*, Fiona Blount." He grins at Gina. "Because obviously I'm supposed to be horrible to you, Gina. So what's the deal—got hot dates?"

Joe's expression goes blank at that. Which is kind of gratifying because if he likes me, he wouldn't approve of me going on a date with someone else. Especially on Friday night, which is a hot date night.

"We might," Gina says, which is not helpful. What if Joe believes her? After that kiss on the cheek I don't want him to think I'm, you know, dating somebody! "Because we are very dateable girls. Actually, we have a power meeting with a captain of industry. Come on, Fiona, let's go. We don't want to be late."

As we walk down the road to the Underground station, Gina laughs and looks at me. "I think that boy definitely *likes* you, likes you. Did you see the expression on Joe's face?" she asks, and I blush. "That's okay." She pats my arm. "You'll tell me when you have less weighty things on your mind. Like William Brown."

As we step onto a Central Line train, I can't help but think that I am only six stops away from meeting my probable possible father!

I am very, very afraid. But also excited.

When Gina and I arrive at Funktech on Tottenham Court Road, my hands are trembling. And when Gina tells the receptionist that we have a 5:30 meeting with William Brown, she calls up to his office, then tells us someone is on the way down to meet us. My legs are shaking.

The elevator doors open, and I get instant prickles. When a nice-looking, plump lady holding a manila file steps out, my heart is pounding so hard in my chest that I think everyone must be able to hear it!

"Hello. You must be Fiona and Regina. I'm Cynthia," she says, smiling pleasantly as she walks the distance to the reception desk. *Cynthia?* William Brown Mobile's Cynthia? "I'm so sorry but Mr. Brown's been called away rather unexpectedly, so we're going to have to reschedule your meeting."

I can't believe it. After everything I've gone through, I'm not going to see William Brown after all!

"I'm afraid he's a very busy man—he only agreed to this window of opportunity today because he had a last-minute opening," she continues briskly as she puts the manila folder on the desk and opens a diary. "Hmm, there's nothing for July. In August, Mr. Brown will be away, so how about sometime in September?"

And all I can think is, *Am I ever going to meet my possible father? All this worry for nothing.*

But we go ahead and agree to a date during the first week of September, even though it means I have to wait a whole three months for William Brown's next available appointment.

Gina fortunately does all the talking and is all businesslike as she makes a note of the date. I can tell by her expression that she's sorry for me. Then, Cynthia offers us the manila folder with some background information about William Brown, so that we can be super prepared for the next meeting. I am already super prepared for *this* meeting!

As Cynthia shakes Gina's hand and says, "We'll see you in September," I get a very bad feeling in my stomach. I should know what's coming next because the prickles at the back of my neck get stronger. When Cynthia holds out her hand, I know that I shouldn't take it, but what else can I do? I take her hand. A wave of energy runs through my body, kind of like an electric shock. I know Cynthia must have felt it, too, because she makes this *oh* sound and looks at me wide-eyed. I let go of her hand instantly and head for the doors, pulling Gina along with me.

When we reach the revolving doors, Cynthia calls, "Wait. Please wait, girls," but I don't stop because obviously she could tell that I have ESP just from shaking my hand, and what about those scientific tests she spoke about? And can I even trust Esper, an organization I know hardly anything about?

Poor Gina is baffled, but she doesn't question my actions.

As soon as we get through the doors, I say, "Cynthia knows about my ESP." Gina nods with understanding and we break into a sprint and run for Tottenham Court Underground station. Once we've caught our breath after all the running, I tell Gina what happened.

"Oh, but how minty that espees can feel each other's power!" she says.

"But what if Cynthia and Esper can track me down via Grandmother Elizabeth? I told them I was her relative in my e-mail. I know I wasn't too specific. And I lied about my age. But I sent that e-mail from *my* laptop, so if they can't track me down via Grandmother Elizabeth, they can certainly track me via my Internet address!"

And now that Cynthia knows that I have ESP, how am I going to ever meet William Brown without revealing my identity? Unless he comes to Mum's concert. That's my last hope. Rock 'n' roll brought him and my mum together. I can only hope it can do the same thing for me.

Look into my eyes, look into my eyes, I think, as Daphne Kat and I look into each other's eyes in the living room. I am testing for mind-reading abilities, but I am not getting very far. Because although Daphne Kat will look into my eyes for ages, that is *all* I can get her to do. Apparently cats do not like to look away first when they are being watched, so it's hardly an achievement.

"It's such a perfect da—ay," Mum sings from the kitchen as she cooks her famous lasagna for Mark Collingridge. "A perfect day to fall in lo—ove. To fall in love with you—oo."

A perfect day. Sure. If you can count confessing to something you didn't do again, plus not meeting your possible father, plus worrying about if Esper is going to track you down.

Mark Collingridge brought his guitar along with him tonight, so instead of me having to entertain him while Mum cooks, he's playing along to her singing. Which is a good thing because I'm not very good company tonight. Mark's really good on his guitar, too. Although he's given me something else to worry about, even if he didn't mean to.

When I got home I just wanted to chill after the day I've had, but Mark Collingridge was interested in what I was doing at school. He noticed that I'd left *Flowers for Algernon* on the living room table. He was only trying to be kind, but he went on about what an amazing book it is and how sad it was. I said I didn't know because I'm supposed to read it this weekend, so Mark Collingridge told me all about it.

Apparently it's about a man called Charlie, who has the same IQ as a mouse called Algernon. Algernon has an experimental brain operation to make him smarter and it works. And because Charlie wants to be smarter, too, he volunteers to be the first human to have it. Anyway, it works on him, too. But Charlie discovers some unpleasant things about people he thought were his friends (they were really laughing at him). Then Algernon begins to deteriorate.

So, of course, now I'm worrying about the experimental drug trial, and although people got smarter and got ESP, are there any side effects? Will I, like Algernon, deteriorate?

Oh, but it would be so convenient if I could read minds, however brief my existence on the planet will be. Then I could read William Brown's mind and solve the problem of deterioration. And of paternity. Plus, I could tell if I was going to be whisked away by Esper to a secret location. If I could read Mum's mind, I could tell if she really is in love with Mark Collingridge. I could read Joe's mind to see if he really likes me as a girl or just as a friend.

"So, what do you think, Daphs?" Of course, Daphne Kat doesn't say anything because she is a cat. But I do wonder if she understands English because she stops her favorite game of chase-the-pen and sits up straight and looks at me. And then she meows.

Maybe she's psychic because my laptop dings and I have an e-mail from Joe!

To: "Fiona Blount" <MarieCurieGirl@bluesky.com>
From: "Joe Summers" <OccamsRazor@sciencenet.com>
Subject: What are you doing tomorrow?

Brian just backed out of coming with me to the Natural History Museum tomorrow (and he calls himself my best friend)! Want to come with me and look at some dinosaur bones? No big deal if you can't.

Still Me
PS. How did the power meeting go?
PPS. Meant to say to you earlier—heard about what you did in English—Marie Curie would be proud.

Oh. My. God.

"Do you think that constitutes a date?" I ask Daphne Kat. And before I can decide what to do, he e-mails me again.

To: "Fiona Blount" <MarieCurieGirl@bluesky.com>
From: "Joe Summers" <OccamsRazor@sciencenet.com>
Subject: Re: What are you doing tomorrow?

Okay, the truth. I so want to see the animatronic Dino Jaws exhibition. It's really for little kids, and I don't

want to look like an idiot going by myself. There will
be a flesh-eating velociraptor. There will be a plant-
munching iguanodon. There will also be several boring
soda opportunities. Go on. Come and look like an idiot
with me. You know you want to ;-).

"I think I deserve some love in my life, however brief it
might be. What do you think?" I say to Daphne Kat, and she
kind of nods her head.

To: "Joe Summers" <OccamsRazor@sciencenet.com>
From: "Fiona Blount" <MarieCurieGirl@bluesky.com>
Subject: Re: What are you doing tomorrow?

You had me at animatronic Dino Jaws ☺.

Chapter 14

"**F**iona has a *boy*friend," Mum sing-songs to me as she comes into my bedroom and closes the door. I'm trying to get ready for my date with Joe, and I didn't sleep too well last night for obvious reasons.

"He's not my boyfriend, and keep your voice down—he'll hear you," I whisper to her.

I *knew* that this would happen. I mean, when I e-mailed Joe to ask him where he wanted to meet (i.e., Notting Hill Gate Underground station), he e-mailed me back and said that he'd call for me. Which is kind of nice, since he lives closer to Notting Hill Gate than I do, which means that he is going out of his way to walk with me. Is this a sign of his possible love for me?

"You've gone to a lot of effort for a nonboyfriend." Mum grins as she crosses her arms. "And is that lip gloss I see on your lips?"

Okay, so it's true. I am wearing a pair of the new khakis she bought me, along with a tight black T-shirt with a diamante kitty face on the front.

"I just want to look nice for myself," I tell her (which is not the whole truth). And then I blush. I was planning on being at the garden gate when he arrived, which would mean no embarrassing Mum moment, but I took too long with my hair. Since I'm going to either (a) get whisked away by Esper, or (b) possibly deteriorate like poor Algernon, I might as well have a good hair day.

"I'm sorry to tease you," Mum says. "He seems like a very nice boy. And handsome. At least you match," she adds, and laughs.

"Okay, see you later." I grab my purse and run down the stairs before she can say anything else to embarrass me.

Joe is in the hall, and the sight of him makes me sigh (but silently). He is wearing khaki cargo pants and a tight-fitting black T, and I see what Mum means about us matching. He looks different—older—than when he's wearing school uniform. And even more handsome (which I did not think was possible).

"Hey," he says, and I am embarrassed again by the admiration I can see in his eyes (but I am also pleased).

"Hey," I say as I reach the bottom of the stairs and pause awkwardly. "Well, I guess we'd better go."

For once, he does not have a "question" for me, and we walk along to the tube station in near silence. It occurs to me that he is feeling as awkward as I do.

"Question, Still You," I say, breaking the ice.

"Give it up, Marie Curie Girl," he says, grinning back.

"Do they really have, like, a full-sized animatronic T. rex at this gig? Because, you know, you promised me a full-sized T. rex."

"Absolutely. It will be so magnificent you will be truly terrified."

"Truly, terribly terrified? But what if it tries to eat me?"

"I'll protect you," he says, which makes me feel all fuzzy inside again. "By the way," he adds, "I like your new hair." And I'm back to feeling shy.

We carry on like this until we reach the tube station. And as we climb onto the train it's so busy that for a minute I think that I'm going to lose Joe in the crowd. He's tall, I'm short. Then he reaches between two people and takes my hand, helping me get through them.

I may never wash it again!

The Dino Jaws exhibition is full of parents and little kids, and we're among the very few teenagers there, but it doesn't matter because the little kids really help us to break the ice some more—we decide to pretend to be ten.

We oooh and aaaah, and I squeal when we see the T. rex, and Joe pretends to fend it off, and we generally goof around. The pile of fossilized dinosaur poo was a killer (mainly because this was the highlight for most of the little kids).

Afterward we go for a burger and soda.

"My favorite was the iguanodon because it was cute," I tell Joe in my best ten-year-old voice.

"My favorite was the T. rex because it was big and fierce and scary," Joe says, and I laugh because he sounds more like he's being strangled than like a ten-year-old boy.

"It was the bestest, bestest, bestest fun in the whole wide world," I say, and he laughs at me. Then he stops.

"For me, too." When he says that we are suddenly teen-agers again. And there is another of those awkward silences, so we just eat.

"So," Joe says, placing his burger on the tray. "What you did again yesterday was—"

"Suicidal? Completely idiotic? Totally senseless?" I mean, I still don't know what came over me. Oh yes, my stupid meeting with William Brown came over me. It was all for nothing!

"No." He laughs and looks into my eyes, and I can hardly breathe. "I was going to say, um, completely selfless. Totally minty, as Gina would say." I think my face is red, so there's no point trying for maximum inscrutability. "Come to think of it, Kieran would say that, too," Joe adds, which makes me laugh.

"Yes, they'd be perfect together." I think we'd be perfect together, too, but I don't say that; I sip my soda instead. And then Joe surprises me some more.

"The, um, other night at Brian and Gina's, you weren't joking about finding your long-lost dad, were you?" Joe asks me. Then, probably because of my completely surprised expression, he says, "I kind of figured it out when I overheard Gina talking about getting a DNA test. Don't worry, though, I won't tell a soul." He reaches across and touches my hand.

And I'm so filled with yearning for Joe that the whole story comes pouring out of me, about how Mum lost my father, and how I found William Brown by accident, and about Gina and my attempts to get to meet him. I don't mention the ESP part, though, because he'd think I was crazy!

"So there you have it. I can't just call and say, 'By the way, did you lose someone important at Glastonbury Music Festival fifteen years ago,' can I? I mean, a guy like him has so many layers of staff in between—what chance do I have to get hold of him?"

"I can see how difficult it is. Especially as he has no idea you even exist. But, you know, maybe you should tell your mother. I bet if she called and said who she was, he'd definitely call her back."

Then I tell him about Mum and Mark Collingridge, and the charity concert, and how busy she is, and does she need an old boyfriend turning up out of the blue after all this time, just when she's getting on with her life? When I explain to him about how I got William Brown to be invited to the concert, and how I wanted to give him the option of, you know, finding Mum if he wants to, rather than me springing Mum and me on him, Joe's all, "I think that's smart." Then, "Your mum was in a band? Wow. Which one?"

When I tell him, he hits his forehead with his palm and says that he should have put two and two together because his parents have some of Mum's albums, and he also knows Mum's name from her music producing because he's a huge music fan.

So that sparks off a whole conversation about music, and what we like, and what we're listening to currently (me: Belle & Sebastian, whom Joe also likes; Joe: The Raconteurs, whom I also like). It's a relief to talk about something else other than my worries!

As Joe walks me home from the Underground station, we are still talking about music, and science, and oh, everything.

Like about his mother, who is a typical mad scientist but in a good way. About how she can't cook, but he and his dad eat whatever she prepares, anyway, when it's her turn to produce dinner. I like that his parents sound so equal opportunity. Who knew Joe was so easy to get along with? When he tells me that he has to talk about Mentoring Minds in an upcoming assembly, he asks me what I think he should focus on, and I'm touched that he clearly values my opinion. And when we reach my house, I wonder if I should, you know, invite him in or something. But would that be too early in our relationship? Will I seem too eager?

"So, Marie Curie Girl," Joe says, looking down at me. "I had fun today."

"Me, too." He's leaning toward me, and I think for a moment that he is going to *kiss* me. But what if I'm a terrible kisser and ruin everything? What if I'm totally misreading this? I look at my feet, instead, and the moment is lost.

"I'll see you," Joe says, and smiles a half smile at me as he turns to go. I think I've blown it. I mumble, "See you" back at him, and watch him leave. But then he turns around and calls, "Here's a question for you. O R R L M C G." And I have no idea what that is, but he's grinning, which makes me feel better.

"No fair. No numbers in it," I call back.

But as I open the front door, a possibility hits me. *Occam's Razor Really Likes* (Loves?) *Marie Curie Girl?* No, it couldn't be that. *Could it?*

Chapter 15

oe and I e-mailed practically the whole weekend. He started out by sending me a silly article about DNA condensing into nanotoroids that look like piles of string (the quantum connection, he called it), along with a picture and a note to tell me how much my explanation of DNA was going to help with Kieran.

So I sent him one about Bob Geldof working on an Internet TV channel to promote world peace. Because apart from peace being a good cause, Joe confessed to liking Bob's music from his Boomtown Rats days. And it just went on and on. . . .

But today it's down to earth with a reality bump. *Practically the whole school knows who I am.* Thanks in part to Peaceflower. But mainly to Mum.

"Fiona, was that your Jane Blount on the TV this morning? I mean, that's your mother's name, right? Did she really used to be in the Bliss Babes?" she chatters in her exuberant way, as she comes bounding across the hall to Gina and me by the lockers before homeroom. Clearly she's forgotten about Total Anonymity in her excitement. "When I saw her, I just thought to myself, she's got to be your mother because you look so much alike!"

I am making frantic hand signals for her to keep her voice down because Melissa and Suzy are also by the lockers and are listening to every word. But Peaceflower just does not get it.

"This is so exciting! My elders really dig the Bliss Babes— they have all of their albums and I love them so! And now they're re-forming! The school band could cover some of their numbers. I must tell Buzz."

"Your mother was in the Bliss Babes?" Melissa looks pretty shocked. "*The* Bliss Babes? You have got to be kidding!"

I am about to say that no, it's another Jane Blount, like I did when they overheard me talking about Madonna, but after all the Friday business I don't, because I'm just a bit fed up. Instead I say, "She's the lead singer and songwriter." The look of sheer incredulity on Melissa's face is priceless. Just for a moment I feel a little pang of satisfaction.

"Unbelievable." Suzy shakes her head as she looks me up and down.

"No it's not," Gina jumps in. "Peaceflower's right—Fiona looks quite a lot like her mother actually. And they are both very nice people." That's pretty strident for Gina, and I smile at her gratefully.

"Oh. I'm sorry." Peaceflower is crestfallen. "I forgot about speaking quietly and not attracting attention, there. I'm so stupid." She looks so woebegone that I tell her not to worry because she'll get the hang of it.

If only I could use my ESP to make the whole school forget about me!

So of course all morning in my classes people kept nudging each other and looking at me, and by lunchtime I just wanted the ground to open up and swallow me. At least it meant that Melissa couldn't try any funny business with me, what with everyone watching me, so I suppose that being Totally Visible has its advantages.

"The key to achieving Total Anonymity is to blend in with the background," I tell Gaynor, Mike, and Peaceflower at lunch, as Stephanie Gordon comes over and asks me if I can get my mother's autograph for her. I tell her I will, as I worry about my fifteen minutes of fame and how it will affect my friends, too.

I can't be with them all of the time. I need to make sure they're prepared.

"Starting first with what you are wearing," Gina says as Helen Johnson comes over to ask when the concert tickets are going on sale. I tell her to check online because the concert's on Saturday and the tickets have been online for a while, but will probably sell out quickly after Mum's TV appearance.

"But we're all wearing school uniforms anyway," Peaceflower says, and I note that she's wearing the awful forest green skirt again, instead of the regulation bottle green.

"It's how you wear it," Gina explains. "You know, keep it as standard as you can. Like if the regulations say white shirt, then don't wear a cream-colored one."

"But a lot of the kids adapt it to suit themselves," Peaceflower says, looking confused. "Melissa wears a dark pink sweater instead of a maroon one," she says, as Melissa stops and says "Loser" to me in her sugariest voice as she walks past our table to Clique One.

"That girl is unbelievable." Gina shakes her head. "She's just jealous because you're famous."

"It's more infamy than fame," I say glumly, as I try to refocus on the important things in life. Like teaching Mike, Gaynor, and Peaceflower to survive school!

"You shouldn't be so down about it, Fiona," Peaceflower says. "I think it's fabulous. *You're* fabulous."

"Not exactly," I grumble.

"Don't worry, Fiona," Mike says. "This is just your Andy Warhol fifteen minutes of fame, then everyone will forget who you are again. Or not," he adds, and I wonder what he means.

"I live in hope." I put down my tuna sandwich. I've lost my appetite. Which is odd for me, because I'm usually starving. "And anyway, Melissa Stevens is part of Clique One," I say to Peaceflower. "She can get away with not conforming. And other stuff, too. As the not-so-popular kids we do not have that option."

"Greetings, famous one." Joe grins at me as he slides his tray onto our table, and my heart starts its usual pitty-pat routine. He has Kieran with him, and I can imagine that Gina's heart is probably pitty-patting, too. "Everyone know Kieran?" he asks, and Gina's face goes red. Then they sit down opposite us. "Can I get your autograph, too?" Joe teases.

"Not you as well," I say, and my ears feel a bit hot.

"This too shall pass, and all will be well." My face gets even hotter because this is what he said to me on e-mail last night, when I told him that Mum had just found out that the segment she recorded was going to be on TV this morning. I mean, they didn't give her (or me) much warning!

"Is that another private joke?" Gina asks innocently, and I know that my face is red.

"I wasn't talking about your mum—you're a trendsetter in your own right, Marie Curie Girl." I have no idea what Joe is talking about.

Then Kieran says that he wants to talk to me about this very subject, too, because it would be a great human interest story for the school magazine. So, although I tell him that Gina, apart from being a fabulously minty writer, knows Mum really well and I'm sure Mum would be happy to talk to her, *I am still not getting it.*

Kieran just says that's cool, pulls his chair closer to Gina, and gets out a pad of paper. Then Joe says to me, "Haven't you heard what happened in fourth-period geography? The birth of the Fiona Phenomenon!"

The Fiona Phenomenon?

"Oh, let me," Brian says as he joins us. "This is way book, as Gina's favorite person would say." Brian laughs, and Gina throws a potato chip at him and flushes because her favorite person is currently talking to her.

"Brian," she warns him, glancing across at Kieran.

"Would you please just tell me what trend it is that I am supposed to be setting?" I mean, apart from setting myself up as a prime bullying target, of course, but I do not say that.

"Apparently, *someone*, and we all know who I mean by someone, uploaded a composite photo of Miss Ethelridge and Mr. Fenton as a background for the school computers. It was a nightmare mishmash of their bodies, arms, legs, and heads.

Melissa and Suzy tried to place the blame on Jamir Pasquale, then Helen Johnson confessed that *she'd* done it," Joe says. "She couldn't have, because at the time it was uploaded she was in French class. Melissa was in computer lab at the time, though, so all evidence points to her."

Oh. My. God.

"But why would Melissa do that?"

"I have no idea." Joe shakes his head. "She wasn't as outrageous as this when I was dating her. Although her mother pretty well lets her do what she wants. Her dad isn't around much, either; he's always at work. She's just not used to being told no."

"Joe, mate, you missed out on the best part," Brian says. "Helen Johnson said that if Fiona Blount could stand up for the downtrodden masses and confess to a crime she hadn't committed to save an innocent person, then so could she."

"You really are a heroine," Gaynor says to me.

"No, I'm not, I just can't bear what Melissa gets away with. I'm still a coward at heart."

"I think you are definitely a heroine." Joe smiles at me in a way that makes me go all gooey inside.

"Well, at least I'll have Helen's company in detention, later." Because, of course, I have to do my catch-up detention for confessing about the Ms. Woods poem.

"Don't worry, we'll all be there with you, too. You are not alone," Joe tells me, and my heart bumps so loudly, I worry that everyone can hear it!

"Excellent idea." Brian nods.

Oh, if only my daughter-of-famous-person and confession infamy would wear off and life could get back to normal!

■ ■ ■

Detention yesterday drew quite a crowd!

As well as Gina, Peaceflower, Gaynor, Mike, Brian, Kieran, and Joe, Helen Johnson's friends turned up, too. I think Miss Ethelridge and Mr. Fenton were pretty surprised. However, I don't think Miss Ethelridge was very happy when Mr. Fenton asked me about Mum and the concert, because she got a funny look on her face and I felt sorry for her. But when I told Mr. Fenton that Mum's boyfriend was helping her out, Miss Ethelridge cheered right up.

"Another important factor for achieving Total Anonymity is to aim for a consistent B grade in every subject," I tell Mike, Gaynor, and Peaceflower as we're walking out of English class. It's difficult to get them to follow my Total Anonymity plan now that I'm Totally Not Anonymous. Oh, the irony of it all!

"Because if you regularly score As, you stand out," Gina adds.

"Then the bullies blackmail you to do their homework for them," Gaynor adds miserably, and we all look at her in astonishment, because she doesn't usually say very much.

"Um, is that what's happening to you?" I ask her. Initially she's hesitant, but then it all comes spilling out.

A few weeks ago Gaynor was checking her e-mail in the computer lab during study period when Melissa and Gang came in. Gaynor was so distracted and in a hurry to get out of there she forgot to log off. Apparently Melissa noticed and sent copies of all Gaynor's e-mail to her own e-mail address, including some personal ones about Gaynor's secret love. Who happens to be a girl. And if Gaynor doesn't do her physics homework, they are going to out her. Gaynor's all anxious that we think less of her, but of course we don't.

"I think you're brave to tell us," I say. "Of course we don't think anything differently about you."

"Yeah, these tactics they're using now are just a front to remind us to keep in line," Mike adds morosely, and tells us that they're blackmailing him, too. "When we were in Mentoring Minds I thought Melissa had changed," he says. "But I was wrong. I made the mistake of telling her about a girl I like. It kind of slipped out of my mouth because she was being so nice to me. That thing she did with Miss Ethelridge and Mr. Fenton? That's what she's got in mind for me and the, er, unobtainable girl."

I mean, this is just so awful!

It's then that I wonder if I can use my ESP to help them. I mean, I'm kind of hesitant about trying to use it, after everything that's happened. I don't really want to risk trying to change Melissa's brain, either, because that would be unethical and what if something went wrong?

"Hey, guys, have you heard what happened in second-period seventh-grade physics?" Joe asks us as we pass him in the corridor. "Lisa Skully and her gang put glue on Ms. Woods's chair and tried to blame it on poor Sara Rosoff. And Janine Finch confessed to it. The Fiona Phenomenon strikes again! See you at lunch." When he said that last part he was looking particularly at me.

So, of course, we feel morally obliged to go and support Sara in detention, too (especially me, as the possible cause of her confessing to a Crime She Didn't Commit). Which disrupts quite a lot of the after-school SACS activities (but means that I get the benefit of Joe's company without having to mentor Bev).

All of these kids confessing to things they haven't done—could this be further evidence of my thoughts leaking out all over the place? Am I really leaking thought vibes everywhere? Is my brain deteriorating as per Algernon? Is William Brown really my father?

Oh, there are so many questions to which I don't know the answer!

Chapter 16

After detention, I know what I have to do. I am going to start getting some of those answers.

Gina and I take the Underground to Victoria Station because I have decided that I have to ring the William Brown Talking Head mobile phone again. Gina insisted on coming in her role as my best friend.

We're heading to the Houses of Parliament for this call. I know the Queen only comes to Parliament on special occasions, but if anyone *was* trying to trace the call, they'd probably think it was someone from the House of Lords or something. Although why I'm worried about this when Esper has probably tracked down at least Grandmother Elizabeth by now, I don't know.

"Just be firm with Cynthia if she tries any funny business," Gina says as we walk down Broad Sanctuary toward the Houses. "And if she asks you if you're really Fiona from the other day, don't say yes. Give her as little information as possible. Oh, you're so brave!"

"I don't feel very brave," I tell her as I get out the mobile. "I feel very, very confused."

"But at least Joe loves you, no matter how long you have left," Gina says quite dramatically because I told her my concerns about, you know, the brain deterioration thing. I wish I could be sure about Joe, too. I mean when he asked me in detention if I'd solved O R R L M C G, I kind of laughed and said I was working on it. I am such a coward! Even though I am trying not to be one.

I take a deep breath, and I call the number. I hope William Brown answers this time.

"Hello, friend, this is Cynthia," Cynthia says, and I am thinking, *Doesn't William Brown ever answer his own Talking Head mobile phone number?*

"Um, this is Anne again," I say because I'm a bit nervous that she might suspect that Anne and Fiona de Plessi are the same person.

"Anne! I'm so glad you called back," Cynthia says, and I can tell that she is. Glad, I mean, because I can hear it in her voice. "What can I help you with today, dear?"

"Well, I'd really like to talk to William Brown," I stress. Gina gives me a thumbs-up.

"I'm sure I can help you with whatever it is that's troubling you," she says gently. "I'm sorry, Mr. Brown's in a meeting— he's a busy man." Too busy for a would-be espee obviously. But this is important. I *have* to talk to him in person.

"Okay. Cynthia, you seem really nice"—I take a deep breath. Then it all comes rushing out of me—"but this is the last time I'm going to call if I can't speak to William Brown. His Talking Head had such a big impact on my life, and I know that he's busy, and you're there to, you know, help him out, and I don't like to give out ultimatums, but that's how I feel."

Cynthia's quiet for a moment, then she tells me to please stay on the phone, she'll see what she can do. And then it happens!

"Anne, it's nice to meet you—even if it's only on the phone," William Brown tells me, and his voice is all lovely and baritone and American. "I'm so glad you called back. Cynthia thought she'd scared you the other day."

"She did?" Does he mean that Cynthia knows that Anne is really the Fiona of the handshake shock? Or does he mean Anne's previous phone calls to Cynthia? "Um, it's nice to meet you," I say, and feel stupid. What do I say to him? "Um, so I've been reading *Flowers for Algernon*, and I was a bit concerned that the drug trial connection might have had some nasty side effects," I tell him. "I mean, once you get the powers, are they yours for life? Even if you are the son or daughter of someone who took part in the trial and you've inherited your powers? Or do they wear out?" Gina flashes me another thumbs-up, which makes me feel a bit more confident.

"As far as we know, they're for life," he tells me. "We only have a few years' worth of evidence, but so far, no exploding brains." I laugh at that. "We don't whisk espees off to a nefarious laboratory for a life of scientific experimentation, either, if that helps. I can understand your being afraid and wary, honey." When he says it, it sounds totally reasonable. Maybe I've been worrying too much. "Cynthia mentioned you might be worried about being tracked telepathically, or via your mobile, but we don't make a habit of doing that, either."

"But it's possible?"

"Some of it. It depends on your particular skills and the strength of them."

I tell him about everyone at school confessing to things they haven't done, and did he think my thoughts were leaking about all over the place? He's not sure if it was my ESP at work, or if all the kids felt that it was a noble thing that I'd done. Incidentally William Brown tells me he thinks it was *very* noble, so I blush a bit.

But then he tells me something else. "Anne, I know you're not sure about Esper, but there is some stuff you have to know. I'm assuming that one of your parents took part in the trial, but they haven't developed ESP so can't help you. You have to be careful. I told you that your powers are yours for life, but there are a few exceptions. Cynthia already told you about overextending yourself. If a person overextends their limit, it can cause harm to them. And until you know the extent, and the strength, and how to use them properly, you could have accidents and harm someone else. Kind of like the leaky thoughts, one action can lead to another unexpected one. Will you promise me not to use them for now? Unless it's absolutely necessary? I'm worried for you."

I'm worried for me now, too, because I don't want to hurt somebody! "Um, I'll try," I say as Gina holds up a piece of paper, which reads, *Ask him some personal questions!!!!!!!*

"Um, Mr. Brown?"

"Call me Will, honey, everybody does."

"Okay, then, Will," I say, which feels weird. "Um, can I ask how old you were when you got your powers, and what you were doing? I mean, did something happen to make them appear?"

"I was twenty-two," he says, and I'm doing the math. That would be the year I was conceived! All good, so far. "I was at a music event, there was a riot, and I had an emotional shock—it seems the powers are linked to emotional events in life—but I was sick for a long time afterward." That would explain why he didn't come looking for Mum. This is definitely a good sign.

"How does that work in the children of espees, though? Do they have to have an emotional shock?" The shock of seeing William Brown Talking Head for the first time certainly had that effect on me! Which is not the whole truth, because I was having prickles for years before that. But the day I saw William Brown Talking Head was when I had my first intense experiences.

"It's quite normal for ESP to develop around puberty," he tells me, which ties in with my theory of why I've been doing low-level Total Anonymity for so long without realizing it. "From what we know, ESP gets stronger as you mature. It's usually a gradual process. But yes, there have been occasions where a strong emotional upset has accelerated the development. It's to do with chemical reactions in the body."

"You mean if, for example, someone found their long-lost father, that kind of thing?" This is a hint. I don't want to say too much to him, but Gina thought I should, you know, plant the idea in his head.

"Is that what happened to you?"

"Um, kind of," I hedge, because I don't want to give too much away.

"Oh, honey, I wish you'd let us help you. You must be feeling a lot of different emotions right now, and that can be a problem with ESP practice. Will you at least meet with me?"

"I . . . I'm not sure," I say. "I think so. Um, are you intending to go to the concert at the Sound Garden in Hammersmith on Saturday night?" I didn't mean to be quite so blunt!

"How did you know about that?" William Brown is startled.

"Um, I just do. Will you be there?"

"I will now. How will I know you?"

"I'll find you. Um, in the VIP area."

Gina thinks there's no doubt about it. He's my father. But whether he wants me is another question completely. There's no going back now. William Brown will be there on Saturday night and he'll see Mum. I'll be able to gauge his reaction to her and decide if I should approach him. I'm sure he won't put two and two together because Mum will be on the stage, and I'll just be some espee girl in the audience.

I am worried about Mark Collingridge, though. Last night when I got home from the Houses of Parliament he and Mum were cuddled up on the squishy sofa in the living room. His arm was around her, and her head was on his shoulder. They were going through the running order for Saturday night and the list of sound equipment they'd need. They looked so cute together. . . . Was I about to Shatter Their Love Forever?

But I can't believe I got to talk to William Brown! I can't believe I'm going to see (meet?) William Brown. Finally!

"Plan your routes to and from school," I tell Mike, Gaynor, and Peaceflower as we're on our way to detention on Wednesday.

I'm giving them more lessons in Total Anonymity. "Keep alert at all times and make notes about the bully's routine so that you can avoid them." I still haven't figured out how we can help Mike and Gaynor with their blackmail problem, but there has to be a way. What would Einstein do?

Anyway, the confessions continued today. Bobby Weston and his gang stuck gum in Gary Gilliet's hair during ninth-grade French. Honestly when will those boys grow up? Joe confessed this time so, of course, we have to support him in his detention. It's not like we can have a Theoretical Stockbrokers meeting without him.

"You came." He grins as we walk into the nearly full detention room, and I catch my breath at the way he is looking at me. A ray of light in my confused world!

"Of course we came," I say, averting my face for a moment, because I'm sure that I have that same look on my face that Mum has for Mark Collingridge. "I'm glad you saved us some seats," I tell him as we all sit down around him. "Because today we are the official Joe Summers support group."

Then I do something really mad! I do not know what comes over me (my love for Joe? my anticipation at meeting my father?). I drag my chair over to sit in front of him, I fold my arms on his desk, and place my chin on them, and then I say, "Okay, Still You. Three W on a T."

He laughs and says, "Three wheels on a tricycle, but I bet you haven't figured out O R R L M C G." I glance at Gina to see if she's noticed, but she's too busy chatting up Kieran, which is good!

"I'm working on a theory," I tell him, blushing. I'm trying to build up the courage to ask him to the concert.

Gina and Peaceflower are coming because in their roles

respectively as my best friend and my new friend I couldn't leave them out. I think Mum was kind of surprised (but in a good kind of way) when I asked her for five tickets (because if I invite Joe, I should invite Brian, too, so as not to be so obvious about My Love for Joe). I wanted to ask for more for Gaynor, Mike, and Kieran, too, but I thought that would be pushing it a bit too far due to it being a charity concert.

On Thursday during English class I get my first dose of tingles of the week. What with everything else that has been going on, I really need another problem! Anyway, just as Ms. Woods is handing back papers from the English assignment we did last week, my neck prickles. My first instinct is to look behind me. So I'm just in time to see Melissa look at her paper.

"This is so not fair," she tells Suzy. "C. Again. I warned that fat nerd that I needed an A this time."

"That's too bad," Suzy says. "You could totally get a better grade if you did it yourself!"

"I could. If I felt like doing it in the first place."

I really think Melissa is losing touch with reality. But she and Suzy whisper for the rest of the lesson. I'm sure they're planning something!

As class ends and we all pack up our stuff, Melissa gets a bottle of water out of her tote bag. It's so busy and bustling that nobody notices when she surreptitiously pours some of the water onto the papers on Ms. Woods's desk.

"Ms. Woods," she says, after she's put the bottle back in her tote and is in the doorway. "You might want to check your desk, because Gaynor Cole just spilled water over your papers."

Ms. Woods looks at Melissa, then at Gaynor. Her face registers shock and confusion. And maybe frustration.

"No, she didn't. I did it," Bev says.

Nobody can believe that Bev has seen the error of her ways and has turned on Melissa. Melissa, for once, is pretty shocked, which is kind of funny to see. Although recently Bev hasn't been hanging so much with Melissa and Gang. Or rather, Melissa and Suzy. And although she completely deserves to get a detention for things she has done in the past, we want to support Bev in her twelve-step de-bully-fication program, so of course we go to her detention, too. Because she is not very popular now that the whole school has turned against the Clique One girls, it's just Mike, Gaynor, Peaceflower, Gina, Kieran, Brian, Joe, and Andrea. Which is another surprise.

"I don't know why you came," Bev says, and I feel sorry for her. "After all, I'm Public Enemy Number Two."

"You have seen the error of your quadratic equations," I say, and smile.

"I didn't do this latest stuff, though. Got it? I didn't have anything to do with"—she glances across at Mike and Gaynor—"really bad stuff."

Do you know what? Despite the attention I've been receiving because of Mum's charity concert and despite the Fiona Phenomenon that is sweeping the school, I'm less scared than I have ever been. Although I'm still worrying about the whole William Brown thing, and will he like me?

And oddly I'm happier than I've ever been. Especially when we all walk home together as far as Royal Crescent, which is where I turn off. And even more especially as Joe turns *with* me to talk about, you know, stockbroker stuff. Or so he says to everyone else. Although I'm still not sure if we're, you know, dating or not.

"So, Marie Curie Girl. Did you figure out O R R L M C G yet?" he asks when we reach my house. Despite being upset about William Brown, the expression in Joe's eyes really touches me. I am standing on the front step and am nearly eye to eye with him. And I think he is going to kiss me again. He has that same look he had last Saturday at the museum. And does it mean, Occam's Razor Really Likes (Loves) Marie Curie Girl? Or am I delusional?

But the front door opens, and it's Sharon, on her mobile phone. "Hello, luv," she says to me, then she's all, "no, I'm sorry but I can't give the minister more than two free tickets for the charity concert. See, that's why it's called a charity concert." The moment's totally lost.

As Joe tells me he'll see me tomorrow and turns to leave, I call after him, "Hey, Occam's Razor. I R T F."

It means I Reciprocate That Feeling. Joe looks puzzled for a moment, then he smiles. I wonder if Joe gets it. And then I take another risk. "Want to come to the concert with me on Saturday?"

"You mean on a date?" he teases me, and I lose my nerve.

"Brian's invited, too. And Gina and Peaceflower," I add, then look at my shoes because I know my face is red. I am such a coward.

"Oh, so it's more like a double date except it's a quintet date?"

"Um, something like that," I mumble.

"I'll be there. I R T F? Bet you I can work it out," he adds with a teasing smile, and then he leaves.

I realize that Sharon is staring at me. "What?"

"Nufink. I was just finking that if I were fourteen again he'd be a hot guy."

Chapter 17

By Friday I am still the Fiona Phenomenon! Will this madness ever end?

So many people are confessing to things they didn't do, too, I mean it's totally out of hand! The detention classes are so full that going there has become almost like a badge of honor! I think, also, that detention has become a breeding ground for love.

Mr. Simpkins and Ms. Maldine were very cozy in detention yesterday because Ms. Maldine finally plucked up her courage (and her mustache) and asked him out. Kind of. Everybody knows because Ms. Maldine's voice is back to booming levels. She said she'd gone ahead and booked tickets for the theater this weekend, but her friend couldn't come with her, so would Mr. Simpkins do her the honor of his company?

We were in detention because Kieran confessed to going on thetruthaboutteachers.com and saying that Principal Darnell wasn't respecting our human rights because of the communal showers. It's true, Principal Darnell really does need to sort out the shower situation, but it was actually Gina who made the post. She said if I could stand up for the rights of our fellow students, then so could she.

Principal Darnell is definitely not impressed, though. He gave a very impassioned speech in assembly yesterday morning about civil disobedience and the irresponsibility of comments on the Web, and if he didn't get a confession we'd all be in detention. The whole school. So Kieran confessed before Gina could.

On the plus side, Melissa has become hugely unpopular. Even the Clique Two crowd whisper about her and Suzy, and at lunchtime only Chaz sits with them. It's like they've become social outcasts and my little group has become Clique One. Not that I believe in cliques, of course.

But there's still the problem of Mike and Gaynor and the blackmail to do her homework. I don't know what to do about that, with or without ESP, because even if I could force Melissa to forget about Mike and Gaynor, or to delete the files, how do I know whether she's got copies on other computers, or on a memory stick, or has hard copies or something? How can I be totally sure she'd forget about them for good? And what if she tries something in the future?

I haven't been trying for low-level Total Anonymity, either. Partly because it doesn't seem to work anymore due to being in the public eye. Plus, I don't seem to feel that low-level fear all of the time these days. Also, I promised William Brown that I wouldn't try anything unless it was absolutely necessary. Which means not trying to expand, you know, Total Anonymity.

Oh, there's just so much to think about! But because I am so distracted by all of the things going on in my new Totally Visible self (plus excitement about the concert tomorrow night), I forget about Melissa and the real threat that she can be.

I should have realized this in Theory of Knowledge earlier, when Mr. Simpkins was discussing alternative medicine, and Peaceflower felt the urge to put up her hand to discuss in detail the eight primary inner chakras and their parallels with the human endocrine system, but I didn't get any prickles. Even though Peaceflower was ignoring everything I'd said about Total Anonymity. Mr. Simpkins was extremely inter-ested in what she had to say, so he spent most of the lesson questioning her. Melissa and Suzy were smirking, but nobody makes comments in Mr. Simpkins's classes.

I guess everything will get back to normal Total Anonymity–wise once (a) the concert's over, and (b) everybody forgets about the Fiona Phenomenon. Thank goodness we only have a week of school until we're out for the summer!

My wake-up call happens in the shower after tennis. The tingling begins just after I remove my towel and stand under the shower, and I look around but I can't see anything except a lot of other teenage girls taking showers. Gina, Peaceflower, Gaynor, and I are doing the towel-clothes-system thing—Peaceflower and I are showering, and Gina and Gaynor are currently looking after our clothes.

Then I hear a not-very-loud voice crying, "Please, please don't do that. Please don't." It's Gaynor's voice.

"Acne Girl, calm down," Melissa tells her. "I thought you and I should have a friendly chat about, you know, the B I got for my physics homework."

"Hey! What are you doing?" I hear Gina call out.

The prickle becomes a huge tingle, and I stick my head around the shower wall, and I feel the familiar lurching in my stomach and faint pressure in the back of my head. *Oh no, here we go again!*

"We just want to try on hippie girl's fabulous skirt." Melissa has Peaceflower's homemade skirt in her hands and is holding it up against herself. "Hmm. I think this is really me, what do you think, Suze?"

"Oh, it's totally thrift shop meets hippie commune. So *not* you," Suzy sneers, but Bev is standing there wrapped in a towel, with a horrified look on her face. Everyone else in the room has the same horrified look on her face. Except for Andrea, who looks as furious as I feel!

"Ms. Maldine!" Gina calls out.

But Melissa is laughing in her face and telling her that there's no point calling for Ms. Maldine because she's just received a fake message that Principal Darnell wants to see her straightaway.

"Oh no!" Peaceflower says, pulling her towel around her.

As my anger and fear build, I am cursing myself for letting down my guard. I grab my towel, too, and step out of the shower, and I don't know what to do. What do I do?

"I'm only being friendly," Melissa says as Peaceflower lunges for her skirt. "I want to look at the craftsmanship. Hmm. Did your mother make this?"

"Stop that," I surprise myself by saying. I've never actually defied her directly before. As Melissa inspects the seams of the skirt, I take a step toward her. "Just stop it!" I shout this time because I'm getting so angry. I mean, after everything that's happened, this is the last straw!

Melissa just laughs. "Yeah, I thought you'd be around here somewhere, with your hippie friend and Acne Girl. You know, you should just stay away from Joe Summers because he's out of bounds. And bad things happen to people who cross me. Just ask Acne Girl or Fat Mike."

The pressure in my brain builds.

"You don't want to get me angry," I say through gritted teeth.

"Oh, did you say something?" Melissa asks as she tugs at the skirt.

"Melissa, you don't want to do this," Andrea says to her. "It's too much."

"Oh, I don't think this is too much. I'd call it too much when your ex–best friend scores straight As and won't help with your homework."

"I said I'd help you with it, but I don't see why I should have to actually do it for you. You just don't get it, do you? You can't control everyone," Andrea retorts.

"Melissa, she's right, you need to stop this," Bev tells her earnestly. "Think about what you're doing."

"Oh, goody, another turncoat," Melissa says to Suzy. "Can you hear crickets chirping?" Then she turns to Bev with a scowl. "You and I are so finished, and guess who's going to regret it more? You, I think, especially when you're not invited to all the best parties anymore. Now where was I?" she asks rhetorically as she refocuses on Peaceflower's skirt.

"Just give it back!" I shout, and lunge for the skirt, but Melissa moves deftly away from me.

"Ooh, I'm so scared." She laughs in my face. "Loser Girl

develops some backbone. It's such a shame that it's only half a backbone, though."

"Nobody here thinks you're smart; nobody here thinks you're cool for the way you act," I tell her as I get even angrier.

"Oh, dear, this seam is a little faulty." Melissa ignores me and tugs again, this time really hard, and it comes apart down the whole of one side. "Oops. I guess it wasn't very well made, after all." Then she throws the ruined skirt at Peaceflower. "Remember what I said about Joe," Melissa warns me.

This just makes me madder. I can't believe what she did, and neither can anyone else. You could hear a pin drop. As she and Suzy turn to leave I'm wishing that Melissa would just DROP DEAD for this. The pressure at the back of my head gets so fierce that I think I am going to explode. I'm just so sick of Melissa and all the torment she's inflicted on people. I really want her to DROP DEAD.

As my vision blurs I see the familiar spots behind my eyes, and a voice inside my head starts screaming at me to STOP. I have to stop! I don't mean that I really want her to drop dead! The pressure is so intense I can hardly contain it. What do I do?

What have I become? Whatever Melissa has done, I cannot go through with this because I do not want to be a murderer! I look around wildly for something, anything. What can I do with the power in my head? Am I going to burst?

Burst? Burst? I focus on the fire alarm on the wall. BURST THE GLASS, MELISSA, I think. BURST THE GLASS!

Melissa freezes in her tracks, turns around, and walks to the fire alarm. She removes the tiny hammer from the wall next to it, smashes the glass, and pulls the alarm. Then she calmly walks out of the changing room.

As the nausea and the realization of what I nearly did hits me, I run back to the shower and puke. I nearly *killed* her!

"That was totally weird," Peaceflower says fifteen minutes later. She's tugging at her skirt, which is actually my spare skirt.

Fortunately Ms. Maldine arrived just after Melissa and Suzy left, and could see that the fire alarm was a hoax. The alarm got turned off straightaway, so we didn't have to leave the building wrapped only in our towels. Which is just as well because I can barely walk, so bad is my headache and the nausea.

Nobody confessed to breaking the glass. I don't know if anybody will actually tell on Melissa, but it would be a lie, wouldn't it? Because although she physically broke the glass, I'm the one who made her do it.

"She's really getting out of hand," Andrea says to Bev.

"Yeah, I know. I don't know what that fire alarm thing was all about. I heard a rumor that her parents were having trouble, you know, because of her mother's spending problems," Bev tells us.

But bad time at home or not, what's really important here is that I nearly wished Melissa dead!

"Peaceflower, you have got to listen to me," I implore her.

My head is throbbing, and I'm really scared. "You *have* to learn to blend in because next time it could be even worse, and I don't want anything bad to happen to you." Which is not the whole truth. I'm also terrified for me because of what I

almost did. "Like wearing regulation uniform instead of that,"
I say, pointing at her jacket and ruined skirt. "Like not volun-
teering answers in class because it makes you stand out."

"It's very kind of you to worry about me, Fiona," Peaceflower
says between sniffles because although she has stopped crying, the odd tear is still leaking from her eye. "But you see,
Pansy would be very upset if I didn't wear the clothes that
she made for me."

All of the frustration I've been feeling is bubbling to the
surface. I have this terrible headache. And I nearly killed
someone!

"Can't you see that your clothes are helping to ruin your
school life? Your mother is ruining your school life! Your skirt
is practically in shreds, for goodness' sake!"

Gina's eyes are wide-open. I don't think that she has ever
seen me this upset. Or vehement. Bev, Andrea, and Gaynor
seem pretty shocked, too.

"And what were you thinking?" I say because I am so angry
with Peaceflower and upset for her and worried about her
(okay, and worried for me) at the same time. "Going on and
on about chakras in class today? You'll never achieve Total
Anonymity if you keep this up."

"What do you mean?" Peaceflower says, sniffling even
more. "I know about chakras. I just wanted to share that with
everyone."

"I know, I know. It's nice to want to do that. But you
shouldn't go around saying that kind of stuff where people like
Melissa can hear it. You stand out too much. You're a prime
target for them. Then you get your skirt ripped in half. Can't
you see that?"

"She does have a point," Andrea says. "It does make you stick out."

"Yeah, you're a bit of a target," Bev adds. I never thought I'd be in agreement with two ex-members of Melissa's gang!

"My elders told me that I should be myself, not a sheep." Peaceflower is now crying again. "If I believe in something, then I should stand up for myself."

"But—but—but not to the extent where it endangers you, you silly girl. And us by association! You have to understand that life in the city is totally different from life on some hippie commune where everyone is all lovely and nice. Real life is like a jungle, it's a fight for survival. Oh, it's totally impossible to tell you anything, because you just do not listen!"

I cannot believe I just said that!

Peaceflower's staring at me as if I have just grown horns.

"It's better than being so scared all of the time that you don't live your life," Peaceflower shouts at me. "I mean, how is this Total Anonymity of yours any better than me being myself? What about the Fiona Phenomenon? Is that just a lie?"

Then Peaceflower bursts into tears again.

Nice one, Fiona. I really am a monster.

Chapter 18

You know, there comes a time when a girl has to ask those difficult questions of herself.

Like, can I ride round and round on the Circle Line on the Underground forever? (To which the answer is no because going round in a circle is not going to help matters.) But I couldn't sleep a wink last night, despite Daphne Kat's comforting presence, and it's soothing sometimes to ride round and round on the tube. Apart from the familiar hum and jostle of the train, you know it's always going to end up back where it started.

Do I really want my life to circle back to where I was a few weeks ago?

What if I really had managed to will Melissa to die? Like how *horrid* of me was it to shout at poor Peaceflower like that? I was completely out of order. I was venting anger when really I was fearful for her.

After Peaceflower burst into tears, I felt like the worst person in the world. I mean, Gina tried to be supportive when she said that someone had to tell Peaceflower these things because I was right about her standing out too much. But I could tell that she thought I'd gone too far. Not only am I a near murderer, I am also a Bad Friend!

Peaceflower is right.

I really have spent so long trying to avoid being noticed, I've avoided living my actual life.

This last week in particular has made me realize that I am so sick of being afraid, I'm just so fed up with worrying all the time. It's time to start facing up to my new reality. I have to stop running away.

When the train arrives back in Notting Hill Gate, I get off and head out of the station onto Pembridge Road. My feet feel heavy, as if I'm wearing weights on them. I turn the corner onto Portobello Road, which is packed with the usual Saturday street market, and antiques stalls, and mystic stalls. It is also packed with the usual Saturday shoppers and tourists, but I hardly register them as I head for the silver and blue door.

Deep breaths. Deep breaths.

I push open the door of Peaceflower's elders' store and step inside. It's pretty mystical, as I'd expected, with crystals, and candles, and jars of herbal remedies and tonics.

"Can I help you, dear?" a woman who looks like an older version of Peaceflower asks me. She is wearing a purple caftan and an orange turban. Yes, this is definitely Peaceflower's Pansy. But before I can say anything, a strange expression crosses her face. She comes over and takes my hand. "Your chakras are very muddled, dear; you've obviously got a lot on your mind. I can help you with that. This essential oil," she says, taking a jar off a shelf, "works wonders to clear the mind and help relieve stress."

"Um, yes, I have got a lot on my mind," I say, touched by her concern for a stranger. And I'm impressed by her powers of observation. I wonder if it is a kind of ESP. "Um, I'm actually here to see Peaceflower, though. I'm Fiona. Um, a friend," I add. Although I wasn't a very good one yesterday, I do not say.

"She's not feeling well today," Pansy tells me, her expression sad for a moment. "I don't think she wants any visitors right now. She had a bad day yesterday."

"Yes, I know. Please. I just wanted to check in with her. To make sure she's all right." I am nearly begging.

Then Pansy totally shocks me by putting a hand on my forehead and closing her eyes. "You feel like a good person who wants to help her heal. Let me go and ask her."

I am also the picture of woebegone misery who wants to apologize to a friend. I don't say this, either, but she disappears for a few moments (which feels like an eternity but is not). Will Peaceflower even want to speak with me after what I said?

But she does want to see me—Pansy takes my hand and leads me through the back of the store to a dark blue stairway, covered in silver stars and mystical runes, and tells me that it's the second door on the right. So I climb up the stairs and knock on the second door on the right, which is bright orange and covered in flowers. It brings an instant lump to my throat because it's just *so* Peaceflower.

When a small voice tells me to come in, I feel my eyes begin to water because it sounds as woebegone as I feel. When I push open the door, the first thing I see on the canary yellow wall opposite is a picture of Jimi Hendrix.

I burst into tears the second I see Peaceflower because she looks so small and miserable sitting on the psychedelic patchwork quilt on her bed. "I am *so* sorry for the things I said to you yesterday. I was wrong, and you were right," I blurt. "It *so* wasn't your fault. I was worried about something else and I took it out on you. And it was very unparsimonious of me. Can you ever forgive me?" I finish, looking at my sneakers.

"Don't say that," Peaceflower says as she jumps off the bed and flings her arms around me, and then she's crying, too. "You and Gina have been so kind to me since I started school here, and you were just trying to help me."

"I was trying to make you a sheep, though. I was trying to make you hide and not really live your life." How could I have gotten it so wrong?

"No, you were trying to help me blend in," Peaceflower tells me as she hands me a tissue from a beaded box on her nightstand. "That's another thing altogether. You were right, this isn't the commune. I had a good chat with Pansy about that last night, and, well, we got some things straightened out."

Peaceflower's mother is taking her shopping for a real school uniform later.

"I didn't tell Pansy all the details about the shower incident, though, because it will only make her worry more." Peaceflower half grins at me. "I told her it was an accident. You know, with my skirt."

"Yeah, I do the same with my mother—I don't tell her

everything that goes on, either." I grin back, thinking of my ESP, and secret fathers.

"Pansy suspects something, though. We had a weird phone call last night, you see"—Peaceflower pauses, then looks at me—"it was someone calling about a birth control prescription for me, which is stupid because I'm obviously not thinking about those kinds of things. I'm too young for that stuff. And I don't even have a boyfriend."

"Someone called about birth control for you?" It sounds like the malicious kind of trick Melissa might play.

"Pansy said it was probably a mistake. Thank goodness, she's the kind of mother who doesn't jump to conclusions about her only daughter." Peaceflower's face is a picture of confusion. "But after yesterday, I think it might be Melissa's work. What do you think?"

"You're probably right," I say, thinking that Peaceflower can be very astute sometimes. "It would seem that she holds a grudge against me, too. Oh, I shouldn't have shouted at you. The only reason she picked on you was to get at me."

"The Fiona Phenomenon." Peaceflower smiles. "For what it's worth, I think you are pretty minty." We laugh at that.

"And you're pretty book yourself!"

Then I tell Peaceflower about William Brown, my quest to meet him, and the arrangement to have tickets sent to him anonymously (but not about the ESP). She stares at me open-mouthed for a few seconds.

"Wow," she says at last. "And I thought I had problems. No wonder you were so upset. But you know?" she continues, almost back to the old Peaceflower. "You have friends and we are going to help you. You're not alone."

■ ■ ■

When I get back home there is a surprise waiting for me.

"You have a visitor, Fabulous Fiona," Mum whispers as she opens the front door.

"He's in there." She nods her head toward the living room door. "I'll see you later," she adds, "at the Sound Garden."

"Good luck for tonight, Mum. You'll be fabulous," I call as she heads down the path.

It's Joe. I pause in the door and watch him as he checks out Mum's CD collection. Then he looks up as he pulls out a White Stripes album and smiles at me. I Go Weak in the Presence of His Beauty. Daphne Kat is sitting right next to him, which is a sign that she likes him. She glances across at me and meows. Her mind is still a mystery to me.

Joe looks up and smiles at me. "Hey, Marie Curie Girl, don't you ever check your e-mail?" he asks as he crosses the room, and he's so close to me I can't breathe.

"Um, hi," I say, confused.

"I was so sure you'd jump at the chance of a trip to the planetarium," Joe says as he wipes his forehead with the back of his hand. "You don't e-mail back, you don't call, and I wondered if you were trying to tell me something. But I guess after what happened yesterday in the showers, you had other things on your mind."

"You wouldn't believe it," I say, looking right back into his eyes. I'm wondering how much he knows. But I know Gina won't have mentioned the ESP connection. I'm also thinking how cute he is, and how much I am not going to let Melissa drive me away from him.

"Gina filled me in. Partly. Want to go for a soda, anyway? You could, I don't know, stun me with scientific knowledge of the Kuiper belt, or amaze me with your grasp of string theory. Or you could tell me how you feel about tonight and meeting William Brown. And I could tell you about Mum's tuna casserole last night, which turned out more like tuna soup. Or you could just tell me about yesterday. But only if you want to."

You know what? I do. "Didn't you know that only weird girls are into string theory?" I tease him as we walk along Holland Park toward Notting Hill. "It's way too mysterious."

Joe laughs at that, then says that he likes weird and mysterious because it's so much more interesting than normal. I tell him that I'm worried about what Melissa will do next and that she'd threatened me. I haven't told him what she said to me, though, about staying away from him.

"There's never a dull moment with you around, Marie Curie Girl," Joe says, shaking his head.

I want to ask him if that is a good thing or a bad thing because, let's face it, who needs a friend (girlfriend?) with all this drama in her life?

Instead, I say, "Well, I used to hate it when Mum moved me to different schools all of the time. Now I'm thinking that it really would be a good thing if she went back to touring with the Bliss Babes, and I had to move schools all of the time. No more Melissa."

"Do you really think it will solve anything if you run away?" Joe asks. He looks very sad about the idea of me leaving.

I remember my resolve. I'm going to face life head on, rather than hide my head in the sand.

"No. I don't think that's a good idea," I say. "I like it around here. I don't want to be intimidated anymore." I definitely like it around Joe.

"That's more like it." Joe grins. "Do you know what you

need?" *A boyfriend?* I think. "You need a plan. How brave are you feeling, Fiona Phenomenon?"

"You know what? I *am* feeling brave," I tell Joe, because it is the absolute truth. "It felt so good yesterday to stand up for what I believe, even though it didn't turn out too well. And I *do* have the beginnings of a plan." This is also true. An Occam's Razor thought has occurred to me. I've stripped the problem down to its bare bones. If you give way to bullies, they always come back and bully some more.

"Why am I not surprised?" Joe grins even more widely, and I smile back at him. "Attagirl. What do you have in mind?"

"Well, your Mentoring Minds presentation next Wednesday in assembly. Would you mind if I hijacked it and *kind* of talked about Mentoring Minds, but *really* talked about something else?"

"I'm intrigued," he says, pausing to look at me. "Tell me more."

"Okay."

As we walk into what I am beginning to think of as "our" café, I explain it to him.

"I think you're on to something," Joe says as we sit at what I think of as "our" usual table. "What are you waiting for? I'll get the sodas, you make the calls."

I reach into my bag for my hot pink, rhinestone-covered mobile and punch in Peaceflower's number.

"Hot phone." Joe winks at me.

I feel like a hot girl. A hot, empowered, grabs-her-own-life kind of girl.

Chapter 19

am still trying to feel like a hot, empowered, grabs-her-own-life kind of girl, but it's hard because William Brown has just entered the building!

I know this, partly because we have positioned ourselves so that we have a good, clear view of the entrance, and partly because I get prickles at the back of my neck the moment he comes into the lobby.

He's wearing jeans and a black T-shirt, and he looks so nice and friendly and approachable. He's glancing around the lobby, and I wonder if he can feel the same prickles as me. His eyes slide over us, then back to the other side of the room.

We've been sitting in the concessions area for the past hour, you know, to scope out the place. And to make sure we don't accidentally miss William Brown.

"He's on time." Joe squeezes my hand. He knows what

William Brown looks like because Gina printed off photos for everyone—five pairs of eyes are better than one.

"Which is a good sign because it means he's anxious to meet you." Gina claps her hands together.

"I think he has good karma," Peaceflower says, touching the emerald green crystal around her neck. It's her karmic crystal, and she wore it tonight especially so that she could help me. I think she and I are going to be friends forever.

William Brown walks over to the concessions counter, and I'm so excited I can hardly breathe. My own father is so close to me that if I called his name, he'd hear me! After paying for his cola, he heads for the main auditorium.

"Are we ready, everyone?" Brian asks as he gets to his feet. I had to let him in on the secret dad story, too, and he was all like, "What else have you got up your sleeve, Ms. Blount?" If only he knew!

"Are you ready, Marie Curie Girl?" Joe asks me a bit anxiously, and I nod. I'm ready.

All five of us follow William Brown into the main auditorium.

He goes to the VIP area, where we agreed to meet. Oh, I hope he likes me. We position ourselves a few feet away from him so I've got a good, clear view.

It feels like an eternity (but in reality is only ten minutes) until the lights dim, and The Child (a new band) opens the concert. They're really good, but I hardly register them because I'm waiting to see what William Brown makes of the Bliss Babes.

David Bowie is also fabulous, but I am so concentrated on William Brown that I hardly notice. Although when David introduces the Bliss Babes and thanks Mum by name for pulling the event together, William Brown kind of jerks and stands up straighter.

I'm holding my breath as Mum thanks everyone for their time and support, and then the Babes launch into "Destructor Toy." William Brown shakes his head as if he can't believe what he's seeing.

"Another good sign," Gina says in my ear. "He's totally shocked to see your mum. If he knew she was a Bliss Babe, anyway, he could have found her easily, so it's obvious he didn't know."

It's time to make my move.

"Are you ready?" Joe asks me for the second time tonight and takes my hand. "Do you want me to come with you?"

"Thank you, but no," I tell him. "This is something I have to do by myself."

I flash my all-access pass to the security guard and I thread my way through the few people standing between William Brown and me. He's so fixed on Mum and the Bliss Babes, though, that when I say (shout, actually, because it's quite loud in here), "Mr. Brown?" he seems distracted. Then he looks down.

"Anne?" He smiles, and his eyes are all lovely and crinkly. "It's great to meet you," he says, and offers me his hand. When I take it, I get that same electric shock running through my whole body that I had with Cynthia. "Yeah, that takes some getting used to."

"There's a lot of stuff to get used to." I don't know what to say!

Just at that moment, "Destructor Toy" ends and Mum's talking again. "Next up is 'Traveling Gals,' especially for my fabulous daughter, Fiona! Fiona, I love you, babe!"

Oh, I hadn't expected for Mum to mention me. It was lovely of her, but it just didn't occur to me. Without thinking, I turn to the stage and wave at Mum.

William Brown looks at Mum, then down at me. "Not Anne," he says slowly as he shakes his head. "Fiona?" I nod, my stomach a bag of nerves and my mouth dry. For an eternity, but which is in reality only a few seconds, he just looks at me.

"I had no idea—" His voice trails off. "But she's your . . . ? And you're . . . ?" I guess he feels just as confused about this whole situation as I do. "I think we should talk about this somewhere quieter. How about the concessions area?"

As we pass my friends, they all smile at me encouragingly, which makes me feel braver. And once we reach a table in the corner of the concessions area, instead of sitting opposite me, William Brown sits right beside me, which is also reassuring.

"I really had no idea. If I'd suspected I had a . . . a daughter, please believe me when I say that I'd have moved heaven and earth to track you down."

He would? This is such a relief!

"Mum tells me I'm her ten-to-twenty-percent happy accident," I say. "So you probably wouldn't even think you had a secret daughter or son. I mean, why would you? You thought you'd been careful, and everything, and it was fifteen years ago. I wouldn't have known about you until I saw the William Brown Talking Head, and I only saw that because I thought Funktech looked like a promising company for my portfolio—that part's the truth, by the way, I only lied about my age in the e-mail Gina and I sent to you. You know—the two teenage investors who came to meet you, then you were called away to something and we didn't—" I stop midbabble. I can't believe I'm talking about birth control and investing with my father on our first meeting! "Anyway, I'm sorry I sprang it on you. I just couldn't think of any other way."

"It's okay, honey," he says soothingly. "I think you were smart to try and find out about me first. I'd have done the same. I just wish I'd met you then."

He's smiling, though, which is a good sign. Then he reaches for my hands. "God, you look so much like your mother," he says, shaking his head. "I can't believe I have a daughter." He squeezes my hands tightly as if he'll never let them go, then asks, "Does your . . . does your mother know about me? That I'm here?"

"Um, no. I didn't want to say anything to her until I was sure that you're really you. You know, my . . . dad." Then I tell him all about how I arranged for him to receive the concert tickets via Sharon and how I procured the rhinestone-covered phone to call him. For a moment I feel totally out of my depth. But I needn't worry because William Brown puts his arm around me and gives me a comforting squeeze.

"We'll work it out. You must have so many questions," he says. It feels so weird to be here, talking to him, that I just nod. "I guess I'd better start at the beginning."

He tells me about the drug trial he and a friend took part in the year he was eighteen because they needed the money for college. But it was cancelled very quickly because some people had a bad reaction to the drug. He and his friend were completely fine, and they never thought for a minute that it would be months (in his friend's case) or years (his case) before they'd suspect that the drug had affected them.

It took that life-changing emotional shock to trigger the effects. In his friend's case, it was the death of his mother, but he couldn't say anything about it to William at the time because William would have thought he was mad.

"As I told you on the telephone, it happened to me during the riots at Glastonbury," William Brown tells me. "I got separated from Jane, and in the middle of the chaos I became very ill very quickly. I had developed a . . . brain infection. I was out of it for a while and had to spend some time in the hospital, which meant that I couldn't find your mother. I did want to find her again," he says, and his expression is so sad that I want to make him feel better.

"Mum tried to find you, too, you know," I say because it's important that he knows this. "She went around to all of the local hospitals to see if they had a William Brown, but none of them did."

"Yes." He nods. "Well, I was rushed to a specialty hospital in London, I was so ill. And when I was well enough, my family flew me back to the States to recuperate.

"For several weeks I couldn't even remember what had happened at the festival, but when I did and when I was well enough, after I'd spent time learning how to use my skills, I tried to track down your mom."

I tell him all about the de Plessi part of our name that Mum forgot to mention and reassure him that if he'd known that part it would have been a lot easier to find her.

Then he puts his hand on my cheek, and I get instant prickles again, and he smiles as I jump just a little. "You will get used to that, honey. Oh, I can't believe I didn't know about you. I can't believe I've lost fourteen years of your life."

"But weren't you ever curious enough to track her down on the Internet? I mean, I know you didn't have that available to you in the early years, but later she was in a pop group, and she was under the name of Blount, so you could have found her via the Bliss Babes website or her production company."

"The Bliss Babes didn't make it across to the USA, so I didn't find out about them until recently. Tonight. About ten minutes ago." He shakes his head.

"It's a lot for you to take in, I know. I've had a few weeks to get used to the idea of you," I say because I want to comfort him, too. I know how he feels!

"But you see, all of this happened fifteen years ago. It was so brief, and time moves on. Life moves on. I have thought of Jane from time to time, always fondly.

"I didn't search for her on the Internet because she would have moved on, too. What if she'd married and had a family? Why would I torture myself with what ifs? Better to leave her as a very special memory and move on myself."

"Mum says the same things about moving on," I say. "Um, she's not married, by the way. But she has a boyfriend." I think I should tell him this important fact because I don't want to raise his hopes, you know, in case he's still harboring love thoughts about her.

He takes my hands again. He tells me that he's engaged to be married, but he's only told his close friends. That makes me feel better about Mark Collingridge. But what if Mum still loves William Brown? I change the subject away from Mum because I'll have plenty of time to worry about her later!

I ask him what happens to people who have the skills and don't find Esper. William Brown looks at me for a few moments before answering. He says that Esper keeps its ear to the ground (by use of secret skills) to help people with ESP avoid attention.

"We have had some occasions when an espee has come to the attention of the authorities," he says, running a hand through his hair. "But we can generally help them to disappear with new identities." He doesn't tell me any details, though, which is kind of worrying, but there's just so much a girl can take in at one time.

Then he asks me about me. Lots of questions about growing up, and what hobbies I have, which is good, because a father should be interested in his secret daughter's past, don't you think? So after I recap the Traveling Years with Mum and life in general, I tell him about my ESP experiences. About the prickles when I know something bad—or something good, like the prickles I get when an investment looks good—is about to happen. He has precognition, too. And the power of compulsion.

There are just so many different kinds of ESP, and he'll tell me about all of them. After all, we've got all the time in the world now. But he's very interested in what I've already achieved. He says, it just takes time to learn to use ESP at will, but there are ethical codes attached to what is and what is not allowable.

Then it all comes spilling out of me. I tell him about everything that's happened at school and Total Anonymity. About making people not notice me in tricky situations. Also, I tell him about the crystal and how I've been using it to, you know, focus. I even tell him about nearly wishing Melissa dead.

"I mean, why couldn't I get people *not* to notice me? Is it because of the Fiona Phenomenon at school, and everyone confessing to something they didn't do, and Mum's concert news? Is it because it's impossible to make the whole school not notice me when I've done something to make myself stand out?" All the time I'm saying this, I'm worrying about how lethal my skills could actually be.

"You," William Brown says, touching my nose, "are one clever cookie. That's exactly why it didn't work. Using the crystal is a good idea, but its use requires training. Cynthia told me you'd asked about that. But, Fiona, you have to promise not to try that again until you've been to what we call ESP boot camp. It's fun, but most important, you'll learn what you need to know about protecting yourself and others."

"I couldn't actually kill someone, could I, just by using my mind?"

"Fiona," he says earnestly. "I want you to assume that anything is possible. *Anything.* You haven't developed your full powers yet, and we don't know the scope of them. The other day on the telephone when I asked you not to use your powers, I was serious. I meant that it can be dangerous. For you, too. You might overextend and—hurt yourself."

None of this is very reassuring.

"What you did with the fire alarm was smart—you recognized that you were in trouble, so you diverted your thoughts—and if you find yourself in a similar situation again, try and remember to do that," William Brown says to me. "But not inward on yourself again—that is not a good idea because you're releasing focused energy directly into your own brain. It has to go somewhere. Normally, once it leaves your brain, it has to travel through the air and it's bombarded by particles before it reaches the brain of the person you're affecting. It's slowed down in the process, but when you turn it on yourself, it's magnified. I'm guessing that because your power levels probably aren't that high yet, you just ended up feeling really, really sick? A worse headache than usual?" I nod, then he adds, "Please, I've only just met you, I don't want to lose you again."

William Brown and I spend the whole rest of the concert just sitting here chatting, apart from when I went back into the auditorium to tell my friends (my friends—what lovely words) that all was well, but I probably wouldn't see them for the rest of the evening.

Gina and Peaceflower hugged me, Brian shook his head and said something about some peoples' lives being complicated, and Joe—he touched the end of my nose with his index finger and said he'd call me tomorrow!

Anyway, it's crunch time. The concert is over, the audience is leaving, Mum is in her dressing room somewhere in the building, totally oblivious to this. *Mum*. My stomach twists into more knots thinking about her, and how she'll feel once she finds out about William Brown.

After everything else that's happened to me, I should be used to this feeling!

I don't want to shock Mum with this backstage, so the best thing to do is to take William Brown home and wait for her. It's weird, sitting here on the squashy orange sofa with him. Daphne Kat seems to like him, though, because she stops chasing a pen around the living room floor, jumps up on the sofa, and climbs onto his lap. First Joe, now William Brown. Daphne Kat is an excellent judge of character!

William Brown tells me about his parents—my grand-parents! He also tells me that he has a sister and brother, and that I have five cousins. All that family I never knew I had! He's just telling me about his house in New Jersey and how I'll love it when I come and stay with him, when I hear Mum's key in the lock.

I run into the hall so that I can prepare her for the shock she's about to get. "Mum, you were fabulous," I tell her as she envelops me in a hug.

"I had a complete blast. Wasn't it fun?" She hugs me back as Mark Collingridge comes into the hall behind her. Oh, I didn't expect him to be with Mum. "I loved every minute of it, but I don't think I have the stamina to do it night after night anymore. So, no worries that I'll be dragging you around on a world tour again or leaving you with Grandmother Elizabeth, Fabulous Fiona."

"Um, well, I might not mind traveling around the world," I say, wondering how to break this to her. "At least, to certain parts of the world, but not permanently. Only on, you know, vacation."

"What *are* you talking about?" She holds me at arms' length.

It's now or never. I take a deep breath. "You know how you lost William Brown by accident?"

"Yes," Mum says, loosening her grip on me.

"Well . . ." I pause and take a deep breath. "I found him by accident. He's in the living room."

To say the situation last night was a bit weird is an understate-ment.

I mean, William Brown and Mum hadn't seen each other for fifteen years, so it seemed like a good idea to let them do a bit of catching up without me around. Mark Collingridge had the same idea. I felt sorry for him because he's loved Mum since their Hamburg days, but she was still pining for William Brown back then.

I know this because after I told Mum about William Brown, Mark Collingridge looked all sad. "I knew this might happen one day," he said to her. "I knew ten years ago in Hamburg that he might come back into your life one day. I just thought that this time we might have a chance." For once, he didn't have a lot to chat about. I felt terrible! And what about William Brown's fiancée? I mean, what if William Brown still loved Mum?

But as Mark Collingridge turned to leave, Mum pulled him into a hug and kissed him. Not on the cheek this time. "Mark," she said to him. "I've already told you how I feel and this changes nothing. I do need to see Will, we have a lot to talk about, but it changes nothing between us. I'll see you tomorrow, okay?"

Anyway, it was pretty weird. Mum and William Brown were like two strangers meeting for the first time, but I guess that's exactly what it must have felt like after so long, and not having known each other very well in the first place.

William Brown said it would be a good idea to keep the ESP secret from Mum, though. In fact from everyone (apart from Gina, who already knows) because the fewer people who know, the safer we espees are.

So after we did the how-I-found-my-father thing (I told Mum I contacted him as a leader of industry under the guise of investment purposes, which is not a lie, but I can't tell Mum the whole truth), I went upstairs to send an e-mail to Joe, Gina, and Peaceflower, just to let them all know I was okay.

Mum was a bit out of sorts last night after William Brown left, although she was trying to pretend like she wasn't. She told me that she's thrilled I've found my father but admitted that she's so accustomed to having me all to herself it'll take a little getting used to on her part.

"Don't worry, Mum," I assured her. "I'll always be your Fabulous Fiona."

"Yes," she said, and pulled me in for a hug. "Yes, you will."

Things got a little sappy from there, but we are having lunch with William Brown today, and amongst other things we're going to discuss me going over for a vacation. I'm going to America! I'm also attending ESP boot camp while I'm there, but that's obviously top secret.

Chapter 20

When I climb up onto the podium in the gymnasium the following Wednesday morning, I am not feeling very brave. Because the entire school is assembled here and they are all looking at me!

I just don't know if I can do this. I really don't. I mean, they are expecting Joe and an update on the Theoretical Stockbroker club, but this is part of the plan Joe and I hatched on Saturday morning. He said that it's a perfect platform for me. I'm the Fiona Phenomenon, he told me. It has to come from me.

Everyone is in for a big surprise, but what will happen if the plan goes wrong? Gina, Peaceflower, Mike, Gaynor, Bev, and Andrea all agree with me, though. I couldn't do this without their approval because they're vital witnesses. I was pretty amazed that they all said I should do this in the first place, really. They have invested their trust in me.

My vocal cords fail and my legs feel weak. Someone (Mike)

murmurs, "Fiona Phenomenon," and I feel a bit better. And then someone else (Gina) says, "You are my heroine," and she gives me the thumbs-up. Someone else (Joe) says, "Go, Marie Curie Girl," and as I see him smiling with encouragement, I step up to the microphone.

Then I think of William Brown, and how I want to make him proud of me.

"Um," I begin, and the sound of my voice echoing around the gym startles me. "Um, my name is Fiona Blount," I say, and someone (Gaynor) cheers. A few more people cheer.

Melissa is sitting in the front row.

As she smiles her horrible smile, I think about what will happen if she's not stopped. I feel a tingle at the back of my neck, and it reminds me of how sick I am of being afraid. But I am calm, I tell myself. No fear (well, only a bit), no strong emotion. This helps me to squash the tingle, thanks to my promise to William Brown.

I glance across at Peaceflower, Gina, Mike, Gaynor, Brian, Bev, Andrea, and Joe, who all helped plan this. If I don't go through with this, I will be letting them down (a friend does not intentionally let other friends down). Plus, I will be letting down all the other downtrodden, bullied masses, according to Mike.

"In business," I begin again, a bit more firmly, "a takeover means one company purchases another via shares on the stock exchange, and today I want to talk about hostile takeovers. I know that sounds boring, and you are probably thinking, 'So, what does it have to do with anything?'"

At that point someone shouts out, "Yeah, get on with it," but Mr. Simpkins shushes them. Nobody messes with Santa's dark mirror image.

"Well," I continue, "it has absolutely *everything* to do with what has been going on in this school over the past week or so."

Someone in the crowd cheers, and the teachers are all looking very confused because this is not part of the program. So I push on before they can think about stopping me.

"A hostile takeover is, for example, when Company Number One makes an offer for Company Number Two. But Company Number Two does not want to be taken over, and therefore makes life hard for Company Number One. It refuses to share certain information with the hostile company, which means Company Number One might be in for a few bad surprises.

"I don't know about you, but Company Number One sounds a lot like a big school bully to me, and Company Number Two sounds like the will of the majority of the school fighting back."

I look at Joe and he nods with approval, and I feel a bit more confident.

"And the will of the majority of the students in this school this week is saying no more bullying. It's time for those nasty surprises for the hostile takeover bullies!" I continue.

A huge cheer goes around the gymnasium, and I have to wait for a few moments before it is quiet enough to go on. And go on I must, because I am getting to the important part, the difficult part. Gina holds up a thumb of approval. She and Kieran are taking notes for the school paper. Then I seek out Joe in the crowd again, who nods and smiles at me, and I take a deep breath.

"All around the school, people have been confessing to things they haven't done because certain people were trying to pin something on less popular students. And just look at the turnout for detentions. I mean if that isn't popular support for no more bullying, what is?"

People are really cheering and clapping now, and I have to say that I am starting to ride the wave! Being Totally Visible is not as bad as I thought it was going to be. In fact, I am kind of enjoying it. Kind of.

"Well, I'm going to tell you about the true hostile bid to take over my life now," I say, which quiets everyone down right away, because everyone loves a True Life story.

"Last Friday, as some of you already know, someone did something mean to one of my friends as a warning to me that they meant business. That someone told me to stay away from another someone who means a great deal to me. I was in the girls' showers wearing only a towel at the time, so you can imagine how upset I was feeling when it happened."

There are a few gasps at that remark, but quite a few people laugh, too, which bolsters my courage. I didn't mean to say the part about Melissa warning me off Joe, though I wonder if he'll get that he's the someone. I look across at him and he smiles and raises his eyebrows. But Principal Darnell gets to his feet and is coming over to the podium, so I know I have to finish this quickly.

"I'm not the first person this has happened to. I mean the blackmail. Because other students are also being black-mailed by this person. One of them because she is gay, which shouldn't be an issue at all, should it? I mean, there are the two male penguins at New York City's Central Park Zoo who've been in an exclusive relationship for years and fostered and raised an egg together." This makes everyone laugh, and Gaynor Cole gives me a nod of approval.

"Another person here has been threatened with a Mr. Fenton/Miss Ethelridge–style pastiche on the school Intranet system if he doesn't do her homework. This has to stop."

Everyone is shouting cheers of agreement. Even Mr. Simpkins and Ms. Maldine. In fact, Mr. Simpkins stalls Principal Darnell and whispers something in his ear, but I have to get this over with quickly.

"Now, what do I do? Do I stay away from the person I like, or do I follow my heart? Because if I let the bully—the blackmailer—win, where is the guarantee that she will leave me in peace? All that will teach her is that she can intimidate me, and I will be a victim for the rest of my school life and probably forever.

"So, I say no. I say publish the photos and be damned. Out our friend and be damned. No more intimidation!" As I say this, the entire gymnasium population goes wild. Everyone's cheering and shouting. Principal Darnell is definitely going to pull the plug on me any second now.

"But," I continue, holding up my hands for quiet, "the person needs to know that I'm not going to reveal who she is because I'm giving her a second chance, here. But if she publishes, or starts outing someone, or tries anything funny on me or my friends again, she'd better watch out. We won't stand for it."

I mean, I could denounce Melissa. I could get her into some serious trouble. But everyone deserves a second chance, especially if they are emotionally neglected by their parents, and are about to be A Victim of Divorce.

"Could those people who are willing to testify, please stand up?" I ask. Of course, Bev, Melissa, Gaynor, Peaceflower, and Mike stand. Joe stands, too, even though he's never been a victim of Melissa's antics. Then Brian and Kieran stand in support, and pretty soon most of the people in the room are standing and cheering.

Melissa isn't cheering or standing. She looks pretty shocked, to tell the truth, and I hope that she's getting the message loud and clear.

"By the way, Principal Darnell," I say, deviating from the script a bit because I am feeling empowered, and it's a good feeling, and I might as well mention this while I think about it. "You might want to rethink those open-plan showers because I'm pretty sure that they violate our human rights."

There is so much clapping and cheering and shouting in the gymnasium that I think I may go deaf. But they are clapping and cheering and shouting for me!

"Thank you, Fiona," Principal Darnell says as soon as he has switched off the microphone. "But I do wish that you'd come to me about this before making such a public announcement."

But you might have hushed it up, I think, but do not say.

Whew. What a day.

People kept coming over and patting me on the back, and saying that they were totally with me, that kind of thing. I mean, it happened in every class! I'm feeling pretty optimistic. Melissa and Gang of One, Suzy, are keeping a really low profile. They weren't even in the lunchroom today. I still feel sorry for Melissa, but she has to understand that we won't put up with her mean-girl ways. We'll see.

Of course, Principal Darnell wanted me in his office right away after assembly, but I wouldn't tell him who the culprit was. I told him that matters were under control, and there was such a thing as being parsimonious with the truth. But if there were more problems, any at all, I'd let him know. Possibly . . .

"So, Marie Curie Girl, what does it feel like to be the most popular person in school?" Joe teases me later as we walk home. "By the way, did I tell you how absolutely fabulous you were?"

"Only about a million times," I tell him. "But you know? My fifteen minutes of fame will pass, and things will get back to a new normal." Whatever normal is.

"Whatever am I going to do for excitement while you're in America?" Joe asks me, and my heart is doing its usual flip-flop in my chest. And then, "It'll be just so quiet without you around to, you know, create Fiona Phenomena in your wake." We both laugh at that. "I'll miss you."

He's got that enigmatic Joe smile on his face, and you know what? I just want to know one way or the other if he *likes* me, likes me. I think he does. I'm going to follow my own advice to myself about not hiding my head in the sand.

"Question for you, Still You," I say, and stop in my tracks. I take a deep breath. "Um, if I were to say to you, M C G R L O R, what would be your answer?"

To say he is surprised is an understatement. But then he smiles that enigmatic smile and takes a step closer to me.

"I would have to say I R T F," he says, getting even closer, and my breathing has gone all funny. "That I really, *really* R T F." His face is so close to mine, and I think that he is going to kiss me. "I would have to say that Occam's Razor Really Likes Marie Curie Girl."

"I Reciprocate That Feeling," I whisper, and then I step up on tiptoe and kiss him. Even though we're in the middle of the sidewalk.

And you know what? It is soft, and sweet, and lovely.

Really Liking is a good place to start.

As I slip my arms around his neck, I'm thinking, *Why was I so scared of kissing? Why was I so scared about revealing my true identity to William Brown?*

Why was I so scared of living my life?

Look at what I have. A gorgeous boyfriend. Caring friends. My lovely mum. And now my missing dad, with whom I'm going to spend time in America this summer.

Oh, and scary (yet exciting) ESP powers, but I'll learn to deal with them.

Could life get any more fabulous?